"I Had A Clue You Might Have Been Coming From A Wedding,"

Beau muttered. "Your dress."

Emily suddenly stared down at her long white dress in horror. "I'm still wearing my wedding dress," she whispered, as if she'd just realized that fact. Then she tugged at one of her lace sleeves, exposing the prettiest bra Beau had ever seen.

The woman was a nut. No doubt about it. But the way she was shimmying was distracting as hell. "Miss—"

Making a husky sound of frustration, she reached behind her and pulled at her zipper. The entire front of her dress fell to her waist, and Beau's mouth went stone dry.

"What in hell are you doing?"

"I'm getting out of this dress, this *wedding* dress," she said. "I'm not wearing this farce, this lie, this *joke*, one minute more."

The woman was most definitely a nut. But the prettiest one Beau had ever seen.

Dear Reader,

I know you've all been anxiously awaiting the next book from Mary Lynn Baxter—so wait no more. Here it is, the MAN OF THE MONTH, *Tight-Fittin' Jeans*. Mary Lynn's books are known for their sexy heroes and sizzling sensuality…and this sure has both! Read and enjoy.

Every little girl dreams of marrying a handsome prince, but most women get to kiss a lot of toads before they find him. Read how three handsome princes find their very own princesses in Leanne Banks's delightful new miniseries HOW TO CATCH A PRINCESS. The fun begins this month with *The Five-Minute Bride*.

The other books this month are all so wonderful…you won't want to miss any of them! If you like humor, don't miss Maureen Child's *Have Bride, Need Groom*. For blazing drama, there's Sara Orwig's *A Baby for Mommy*. Susan Crosby's *Wedding Fever* provides a touch of dashing suspense. And Judith McWilliams's *Practice Husband* is warmly emotional.

There is something for everyone here at Desire! I hope you enjoy each and every one of these love stories.

Lucia Macro

Senior Editor

Please address questions and book requests to:
Silhouette Reader Service
U.S.: 3010 Walden Ave., P.O. Box 1325, Buffalo, NY 14269
Canadian: P.O. Box 609, Fort Erie, Ont. L2A 5X3

LEANNE BANKS
THE FIVE-MINUTE BRIDE

SILHOUETTE *Desire*

Published by Silhouette Books

America's Publisher of Contemporary Romance

SILHOUETTE BOOKS

ISBN 0-373-76058-2

THE FIVE-MINUTE BRIDE

Copyright © 1997 by Leanne Banks

This edition published by arrangement with Harlequin Books S.A.

® and TM are trademarks of Harlequin Books S.A., used under license.
Trademarks indicated with ® are registered in the United States Patent
and Trademark Office, the Canadian Trade Marks Office and in other
countries.

Printed in U.S.A.

LEANNE BANKS

is a national number-one bestselling author of romance. Recognized for her sensual writing, with a Career Achievement Award from *Romantic Times* magazine, Leanne likes creating a story with a few grins, a generous kick of sensuality and characters that hang around after the book is finished. The "How To Catch a Princess" trilogy was inspired by Leanne's memories of her childhood and is set in Roanoke, VA, where Leanne grew up. Leanne loves to hear from readers. You can write her at P.O. Box 1442, Middletown, VA 23113.

A big smile and cheer for all the sandbox princesses, especially those who got their start on Pawling Street in Roanoke.

This book is dedicated to my favorite feminine wonder who makes my life so rich—Alisa Anne Banks. How did I ever get so lucky to have such a wonderful daughter?

Prologue

When Emily St. Clair grew up, she wanted to be a cowboy. A loud cowboy with a big black hat, one of those fringed jackets and noisy boots. She wanted a horse named Black Devil, too.

But right now she was only an eight-year-old girl with blond hair, a pink-and-white shorts set and a too-tight ponytail with a pink satin ribbon. Her poodle's name was Teenie.

Her mom always said it was best to be practical. If Emily couldn't be a cowboy today, she supposed she'd just be a princess. She looked down at the box of play clothes on the ground. It was a typical spring day on Cherry Lane. The birds were chirping, the bees were buzzing, and she and her friends had to play at the fence because Maddie was grounded again.

"Can I have the red ones this time?"

Emily nodded and handed her mother's red high heels over the chain-link fence to Maddie Palmer. She tugged at the pink satin bow her mother habitually put in her hair. Emily liked Maddie because she was loud. "What are you in for this time?"

Red-haired Maddie made a face. "I took a grape Popsicle without asking and told Ben he could have half of it if he wouldn't tell Mama. But the little twerp got purple all over his shirt, so he had to tell." She shook her head. "Brothers!"

Emily didn't have a brother or sister, so she just wiggled her shoulders the way she'd seen the older kids do it. Then she turned to ten-year-old Jenna Jean who was sitting on the ground and making whistling sounds with a blade of grass. "Do you want the black shoes or the white ones this time?"

"I'll take the white," she said, and began to untie her tennis shoes.

Emily set the heels down beside Jenna. New to the neighborhood, Emily feared the only reason the older girls let her play was because she had three pairs of high heels to share with friends.

If the shoes didn't impress the kids on Cherry Lane, then the tiara did.

Her mother had a ton of them because she used to win beauty contests, so she'd given Emily one of her crowns. She tugged at her ribbon again and wished her mother wouldn't make her ponytail so tight.

Jenna Jean squinted her eyes at Emily. "How come you always wear a pink ribbon?"

Emily sighed. She'd asked her mother the same

question a zillion times. "My mother likes pink. Are we going to play princesses again?"

Jenna Jean stood and stuck her feet into the high heels. "I don't want to play princesses."

Emily tamped down her disappointment and remembered her mother had said she'd make friends more easily if she played what they wanted to. "Okay. We can pretend we're grown-ups. We can pretend we're married and we're rich and we have to order our servants around all day long."

"Yeah," Maddie said with enthusiasm. "When I grow up, I want to marry Davey Rogers from the Pink Bubblegum Rockers."

"He's too old," Jenna Jean said.

"He is not," Maddie said adamantly. "He's just nineteen."

Jenna Jean rolled her eyes. "Well I don't want to get married."

Emily and Maddie looked at her in shock.

"I don't," she insisted. "Boys are dumb, and my mother's always complaining about my dad's underwear on the bathroom floor. When I grow up, I want to get rich all on my own and live by myself and not have to share my room with anybody."

Everybody knew Jenna Jean had five younger brothers, and they were always getting into Jenna Jean's stuff. "Okay," Emily said, although she wished she had a brother or sister or just *somebody* besides her mom and Teenie.

Since her dad died two years ago, they'd had to move, and her mother made so many rules that sometimes Emily got a headache thinking about all of them.

Just yesterday, her mom had told her about the charm classes at the local department store. She sighed and decided to think about that when she took her bath tonight. Sitting in a bathtub made it easier to think about things that bothered her. Even though she wanted to wear the tiara today, she gave it to Jenna Jean. She really wanted the girls to like her. "You could be a rich and famous movie star," she suggested.

"That's cool." Grinning, Jenna Jean stuck the tiara on her head and pulled a fake stole around her shoulders.

"And I'll pretend me and my husband are rich and famous rock stars." Maddie pulled her shirt down to bare one shoulder and made a sneer. She glanced at Emily. "What are you gonna be?"

Squelching her secret, secret fantasy along with her wish to never wear another pink satin ribbon, Emily was practical. "I'm going to be a doctor's wife," she said decisively, and put her nose in the air like she thought a snooty person would. "My mom says if you marry a doctor, you're set for life."

One

Beau lost the coin toss.

Jimmy's face split into a wide grin. "You get to address the little problem over there in the corner."

Beau Ramsey sighed and glanced around the nearly empty bar. Officially off duty, he was beginning to think he should wear a sign announcing that fact to the world. Right now he should be home nursing a beer watching the baseball game he'd taped earlier. "Technically this is a matter for the business owner to handle. You don't need the sheriff."

"She's drunk 'n' disorderly."

Beau glanced over at the little problem in the corner. "Drunk," he agreed. "Not necessarily disorderly."

"Just give her time," Jimmy said knowingly. "She's been knocking back tequilas for two hours.

She's either gonna get disorderly or she's gonna fall on her face." Jimmy gave a meaningful glance at his watch. "It's closing time, and Thelma's waiting for me."

Stifling a groan, Beau took another swallow of his beer and studied the little problem taking up space in The Happy Hour Bar. Pretty and blond, she was dressed in yards of white satin and lace that suspiciously resembled a wedding dress. From her painted nails to her satin pumps, she was a vision of feminine class. Her BMW was parked in the gravel lot. According to Jimmy, the only words she'd uttered had been "Tequila, please," and "Thank you."

There was a story here, and Beau was convinced he didn't want to hear it. As a man who'd been surrounded by women his entire life, he could tell this one was in extreme distress. Unfortunately, as the primary lawman in the rural town of Ruxton, North Carolina, he was asked to address some pretty outrageous situations. "You owe me for this one, Jimmy."

Jimmy whipped his towel over the counter again. "Put it on the tab."

The tab was endless. Beau had been pulling Jimmy out of scrapes since elementary school. He rose from the stool and walked to her side. "Excuse me, ma'am."

Her blurred blue gaze rose to his. "Yes, sir," she said in a husky voice.

Beau's lip twisted at the way her sexy tone mixed with the polite words. Her skin was flawless, her cheeks pink, her lips slightly parted. Her white dress drooped over one shoulder, revealing the shadow of her cleavage. Tendrils of blond hair escaped from what he guessed had once been a classic knot.

A dozen questions came to mind, starting with "Why aren't you in the honeymoon suite of a hotel with some lucky man?" and "Who's the poor sap that isn't going to see what's underneath all that lace?"

A shot of pure masculine curiosity thudded through his veins. Deliberately lifting his gaze from her breasts, he cleared his throat. "It's closing time. Do you need to call someone to take you home?"

She wrinkled her brow. "Home?"

"Yes. You've had too much to drink, so you can't drive."

She looked around and swept the skirt of the dress to one side to lean closer to him, then whispered, "Are you suggesting that I'm drunk?"

If he lit a match near her mouth, her breath would probably set the place on fire. For an insane moment he suspected that in a different situation her mouth would set a man on fire. He stifled a curse.

"Yes," he finally said, noting the pink garter just above her knee. "I am."

"Oh, my." She bit her lip, and Beau felt a tinge of sympathy despite his ongoing vow to remain unaffected by women in distress. "Where am I?"

Beau's hopes sank. She was worse than he'd thought. "Ruxton, North Carolina."

She looked at him blankly.

"Where do you live?"

She shook her head vehemently, then clutched her forehead as if the movement had been painful. "I'm not ever going home again. Never, ever. Not in a million—"

Beau lifted his hands. "Fine, but you've got to stay somewhere tonight."

"Why can't I get a room here?"

"Because there aren't any rooms here, Miss—"

"Emily," she told him, in that soft sexy voice that threatened his neutrality. "My name is Emily."

"And your last name?"

She frowned for a long moment. "I'm not sure." She grimaced. "I've never had this much tequila before. My stomach hurts."

"That's not the only thing that's gonna hurt," he muttered. "Okay, let's get you out of here." He offered his hand.

Emily took it and rose unsteadily. The woman was too trusting, Beau thought with disapproval, but he supposed her judgment was impaired.

"Where you takin' her?" Jimmy asked as he opened the heavy wooden door.

"I don't know," Beau said darkly. "My sisters' houses are crammed full with kids. It'll either have to be my house or the jail."

Jimmy shook his head. "She don't look like the jailbird type."

Beau just swore as Emily leaned against him, the soft floral scent of her hair rising to his nostrils. He urged her into the quiet night toward his Jeep.

"Today was my wedding day."

"You don't say." Beau glanced at her and felt another sinking sensation. He wasn't surprised. A beautiful married woman. This was not his lucky night.

Emily nodded solemnly. "He was a doctor." Her face tightened. "But he loves somebody else, so I left. My mother will have to be sedated. I'm never going back. Never, ever."

"I had a clue you might have been coming or going to a wedding," he muttered. "Your dress."

Emily jerked to a stop and stared down at her long white dress in horror. "I'm still wearing my wedding dress," she whispered, as if she'd just realized that fact.

Beau shot her a wary glance. "Yeah."

"I can't do this anymore," she said to herself. "I just can't—" She tugged at one of her lace sleeves, then shoved one of the satin shoulders halfway down her arm, exposing the prettiest strapless bra Beau had ever seen. It was so low it revealed the tops of her rose-colored nipples.

The woman was a nut. No doubt about it. But, sweet Peter, the way she was shimmying was distracting as hell. Beau shook his head and cleared his throat. "Miss—"

Making a husky sound of frustration, she reached behind her and started to pull at her zipper. The entire front of the dress fell to her waist and Beau's mouth went stone dry. Her breasts were plump, high, and the baser part of him was praying she would keep wiggling until they escaped the confines of her bra. He felt as if his brain had just plunged into his jeans and all he could do was stare.

The sound of an engine backfiring down the road snapped him out of his fantasy. "What in hell are you doing?"

She continued to squirm, mesmerizing him with her movements. "I'm getting out of this dress, this *wedding* dress," she said.

The woman was most definitely a nut. It went against every bit of testosterone in his body to prevent an attractive women from undressing, but someone had to lend sanity to this situation. Beau put his hands on her arms and tugged the satin dress upward. "You can't take the dress off. You're in a parking lot. A public parking lot."

Adamant, Emily pushed his hands away and her dress back down. "I don't care. I'm not wearing this farce, this lie, this *joke* one minute more."

Beau swore and jerked the dress up again, this time keeping his hands on the satin. "Just keep it on until I get you home."

She shook her head and tugged at the same time he did. "No!" A tearing sound permeated the darkness. She froze. "Oh, no."

Beau saw the stark distress in her wide eyes and felt his gut dip. He'd torn her wedding dress, for Pete's sake. *Oh, no.* She was going to cry. He cringed. He hated it when women cried. "Listen, it'll be okay. You'll—"

She shook her head and gave him a desperate look. Her face went pale. "Excuse me, but I think I'm going to be—"

Then Miss Emily lost her tequila on his boots.

The bride from hell slept late the following morning.

After a quick shower, Beau checked on Miss Emily

and sighed impatiently. Sunday morning was a great morning to sleep in and wander around the house in his underwear. His unexpected visitor, however, had nipped those plans in the bud.

Emily might look like an angel, but his boots knew better. He'd sprayed them with a water hose at Jimmy's, then driven home. It was tough to hold a grudge, however, when the woman expressed her apologies every other minute. After he'd directed her to his bed, the only *real* bed in his house at the moment, he'd crashed on the sofa which was about a foot too short for his long frame.

Beau liked his solitude. He liked messing up his dishes and not having anyone gripe at him. Drinking a beer and smoking a cigar alone in the privacy of his home was one of his top-ten most relaxing things to do. It wasn't that he was a hermit or misogynist. He appreciated women, the sound of their voices, their bodies, the way they walked. Hell, he loved the way they smelled and breathed.

But Beau had learned through hard personal experience that associations with the female gender were best conducted in controlled doses. Convinced that many of his buddies' main problems stemmed from overexposure to estrogen, the only female he allowed around him on a regular, twenty-four hour basis was his black lab, Cookie. Unlike his beloved but bothersome sisters, she was quiet and easy to please.

Sipping his coffee, he scowled at the woman sleeping peacefully. He was irritated because he'd missed his ball game, his boots would never be the same and he had a crick in his neck. All thanks to Miss Emily.

He looked at her critically. Even in sleep with her hair mussed and her makeup smudged, she was pretty.

She was pretty, but she was a pain.

Her body completely still, she surprised him when her big, blue eyes fluttered open and her gaze latched onto his.

"You're not Carl." Emily said the first words that came into her pounding head as she looked at the big frowning stranger in the doorway.

His expression didn't change. "I'm Beau Ramsey. You're in my bed."

Alarm shot through her and she quickly sat up. Her head screamed in protest and her stomach wrenched. "Oh, my, what—where—"

She clutched her forehead and took deep breaths. When she was able to open her eyes, she noticed the white lace around her wrist. She was still wearing her wedding gown. Her stomach sank further as a flood of disorganized memories rushed through her.

Her wedding had been yesterday. Of course she'd left midway through the ceremony. The shocked faces of her fiancé, mother, bridesmaids, and all three hundred and fifty-four wedding guests crowded her mind.

Along with the imposing presence of the unhappy man in the doorway.

He didn't look at all like Carl. Carl was tall but thin, with a fair complexion and prematurely receding hairline which she'd insisted she never minded. Carl was elegant and refined.

On the other hand, this man was uncivilized looking. Everything about him was dark, from his full head of black hair to his dark eyebrows and brown eyes to his forbidding scowl. His casual shirt was stretched across broad shoulders and failed to conceal well-developed biceps. Her gaze dropped to his jeans and she blinked at the way the denim molded his hips and thighs with heart-stopping accuracy.

The physical package was threatening enough, but the way he stood watching her, with casual, masculine ease and more confidence than any human should possess shredded her already tattered nerve endings.

Gutless wonder that she was, Emily saw the vast potential for panic in this situation. If she wasn't afraid that it would split her head in two, she might scream, but she suspected she would need every bit of brainpower she could muster with this man.

She swallowed. "Please pardon me. I'm not at my best this morning, and there are a few gaps in my— uh—short-term memory."

He nodded. "You were knockin' back tequila last night at the Happy Hour Bar until you were drunk on your a—"

He must have seen her eyes widen in alarm. Clearing his throat, he altered his tone. "Until you became incapacitated. Since I'm the sheriff of Ruxton, North Carolina, I'm often called in for this kind of insanity, even," he added in a tone oozing resentment, "on my nights off."

"Oh," Emily said, and more pictures came to mind. She remembered the rustic bar and her original plan to get a soft drink. Depression had taken over, however, when she realized she was spending her wedding night in a bar. She didn't recall much of her conversation with the sheriff. Unfortunately she did recall getting sick on his boots.

Emily closed her eyes again, this time in embarrassment. "I'm very sorry about your boots. I'll be glad to replace them."

"All starting to come back to you?" Beau prodded.

"Yes," she whispered full of disappointment and shame.

"Then I reckon you've learned an important lesson, Emily," he said, his voice stabbing her consciousness like black coffee.

An important lesson? Just one? How about ten! She couldn't begin to catalog everything she'd learned in the last twenty-four hours. She peeked at him between her fingers. "What important lesson?"

"Tequila's a helluva lot better going down than coming back up."

Emily blinked. Her life was completely devastated and this man was talking about tequila. "How profound," she said, and lowered her hands to look at him. His gaze unsettled her. Behind his easy confidence, there was an intensity about him that made her uncomfortably aware of the fact that she was in his bed.

Emily suspected that when a woman woke up in Beau's bed, she rarely woke up alone. And she'd bet her mother's diamond tiara that whoever he chose to take to his bed never woke wearing a stitch of clothing. If he didn't remove her clothes with his hands, he could probably burn them off with his hot gaze.

Her stomach gave a jolt and she decided it might be best if she got out of bed. Clearing her throat, she pushed off the covers and slid her feet to the floor. Her head pounded and her stomach twisted with nausea. She lifted her hand to her forehead.

Beau stepped toward her. "You gonna be sick?"

She shook her head and winced at the motion. "No. I just—" She took a deep breath and smelled the shower-clean scent of him. She kept her gaze averted, and frowned when she saw the rip in her dress. "When did that happen?"

"What?"

She pulled at the torn seam. "This? I don't remember—" She broke off and made a frustrated sound.

"You really don't remember how it happened?" he prompted.

Her mind drew a blank. She looked up at him and shook her head. "No."

He nodded. "Okay."

Emily waited for him to explain, but he remained silent. "Are you going to tell me?"

He gave her a considering glance and shook his head. "Nah," he said, and turned to leave the room.

Surprised, she stumbled after him, wondering how his easy stride ate up so much space. Must be his long legs. "But you know...when it happened."

"Yeah. Do you want some coffee before I take you to get your car?"

She stepped in front of him. "I'd like to know how this dress was torn."

His gaze swept over her breasts, then back up to her eyes. "No, you don't."

Irritated and more than a little rattled, she thought of all the times she'd been told what she wanted and what she didn't want. Emily stiffened her spine. "Yes, I do."

He gave her a long assessing glance, then shrugged. "You tried to strip in the Happy Hour Bar parking lot last night and I *prevented* you."

Emily gaped at him. "That's impossible. I don't believe you. You tore my dress!"

"You were pushing it down. I was pulling it up."

"You're crazy."

He lifted a dark eyebrow as if he was certain *she* was the one with one sandwich short of a picnic. "You said, 'I'm not wearing this farce, this lie, this joke one minute more.'" His gaze dropped to her breasts. "And your strapless bra has two little white roses right in the middle."

Emily blinked, his words echoing through her mind. They sounded familiar. *Farce, joke, lie.* Her stomach rolled. "I didn't *really* try to undress in a public parking lot, did I?" she whispered.

"Yeah, you did. And next time you decide to strip, Emily, don't expect me to stop you."

A knock sounded at the door. "Oh, Beau," a singsong feminine voice called. "Jimmy's wife called Valene and she called Rosemary, so we—"

Beau swore and looked at the ceiling as if he needed help. "Just a minute. Just a minute," he called, then turned to Emily. "It's my sisters. If you want to get out alive, you better hide in the bathroom."

"Bathroom?" Emily echoed.

"At the end of the hall."

"Oh, Beau," the singsong feminine voice called again.

Beau swore again. "Better get the lead out, Emily, the bridal party's almost here. Hell, this day's gotta get better. It can't get worse." He strode toward the kitchen.

"Down the hall," he told Emily, and braced himself for the invasion. Hearing the click of the bathroom door, he jerked open the side door to his house and calmly greeted his sisters. "Good morning. This is not an approved time for visiting your brother."

Rosemary looked hurt. Valene widened her eyes as if she hadn't a clue about his comment. Caroline just smiled and shoved through the doorway. "Oh, you!" she said and jabbed him in the ribs with her elbow. "We usually leave you alone in the mornings in case you've got a visitor, but this one's different. She was wearing a wedding dress, and everybody knows no woman in a wedding dress has gotten within five miles of you."

Beau watched his three wily sisters work their way into his den. Rosemary straightened a picture. Valene plumped a pillow. Caroline plopped down in his favorite chair.

He squinted his eyes to keep them from twitching. "It was part of the job. The woman was incapacitated."

Valene nodded. "Jimmy said she was a pretty thing."

"I heard she was drinking straight whiskey," Rosemary added.

Beau restrained the urge to correct her. "She was just passing through."

Caroline sat up. "She can't be gone. Her BMW is still in Jimmy's parking lot."

"She's just passing through," he said firmly.

The sound of running water coming from the bathroom may as well have been a stage whisper. In unison his sisters perked up.

"She's in the bathroom," Rosemary said triumphantly.

Beau ground his teeth together and watched Valene adjust a lamp shade. He just hoped his sister didn't go fishing in the drawer on the end table where she'd find where he kept his cigars. Best to get Emily out in the open. "Come on out, Emily," he called, then added dryly, "My sisters are dying to meet you."

He heard the doorknob rattle and her footsteps on his oak hallway. Hearing his sisters' gasps, he glanced up and felt a punch in his gut. She'd washed her face and released her shoulder-length golden blond hair from its knot. The only evidence of last night's excess was her pale complexion. Her blue eyes looked huge, her rose mouth was parted slightly. Her hand clutched the tiara veil. Dressed in the elaborate white gown, she looked like a—

"She looks like a princess," Rosemary whispered.

Emily's lips tilted into a wry smile and she shook her head. "I think I'm ready to hang up my crown."

Caroline tossed Beau an inquiring look. "Where'd she sleep last night?"

The question put color in Emily's cheeks. Beau rolled his eyes. "She got the bed. I got the sofa."

Valene stepped closer. "The gown. It's Dior, isn't it?"

"Yes," Emily said, and her mouth tightened in a firm line. "Do you know someone who could use it? It has a tear, though…"

Valene lifted her hands to her cheeks in amazement. "But it's your wedding dress. A Dior," she repeated.

"Was my wedding dress," Emily corrected. "I won't be needing it after I get to the suitcase in my car."

That announcement left his sisters speechless for a moment. He could sense their combined curiosity swell. Beau saw the flicker come and go in Emily's eyes, anger and womanly determination, and he felt an alarm go off inside him. He had an instinct for identifying potential problems. It served him well in his capacity as sheriff. And as a man. He'd seen that expression before, the look of a lady pushed too far, the expression of a good woman ready to go *bad*. Give well-bred, soft-spoken, classy Emily a little time and she would wreak havoc. Underneath that white lace, she was dangerous. He would just as soon she do her wreaking somewhere other than Ruxton.

Caroline stood, continuing to give Emily an assessing gaze. "We'll take you to your car. Beau says you're just passing through, but Ruxton's a friendly place if you think you'd like to stay awhile."

Emily lifted her hand to her forehead. "I hadn't really decided what I was…" She grimaced. "Is there a hotel?"

"No," Beau said, quickly, firmly.

Rosemary shot him a dirty look. "You could stay with one of us until you find a place to rent."

Beau bit back an oath. He'd seen his sisters do this

before. Take in a stranger as if she was a lost puppy. The action was partly motivated out of the goodness of their hearts and partly motivated out of sheer nosiness. "Emily may not find Ruxton's atmosphere to her liking."

"Why not?" Valene asked.

"I don't think she's the kind of woman who'd be happy living in a place where the primary entertainment on Saturday nights is a tractor-pull race."

"You don't know about her background, do you?"

"I can guess," he told Rosemary. "She probably went to a private liberal arts college and majored in something like English."

His sisters looked at Emily expectantly.

"Fine art," Emily corrected. "I have a master's degree in fine art."

Beau nodded. "And are you employed?"

Emily cleared her throat. "I've primarily been involved with charity work for the last six months."

Beau's lips twisted in satisfaction.

"There's no need to be nasty," Caroline said. "Why don't we ask Emily what she wants to do?"

All eyes turned to Emily.

She blinked as if she'd never been asked her preference. Then her face cleared, and she smiled so brightly Beau would have sworn he didn't need any lights in his room. "I want to get out of this dress, and I want to stay."

Two

Emily St. Clair was wreaking havoc by the following week.

"It hurts me," Jimmy said to Beau. "But I'm not sure I'm gonna be able to keep her."

"What's the problem?" Beau asked, glancing at Emily as she worked the other end of the bar. "She can't remember the beer orders?"

Jimmy shook his head. "No. She's smart enough. It's the customers and, uh—" he lowered his voice "—Nadine. I had Emily waiting tables, but she kept getting offers."

"Kept getting hit on," Beau clarified as he sipped his beer. He wasn't surprised. If he didn't have that itchy instinct warning him away from her, he might be making a few indecent proposals himself.

"No. She kept getting marriage proposals."

Beau choked. "Are you joking?"

"No. These guys wanna take her home to mother and then to bed or vice versa. Anyway, I put her behind the bar to kinda, you know, protect her a little." Jimmy sighed. "The damn bar's packed now. And Nadine's pissed because her tips have dropped down to nothing."

Beau looked at the crowd around the other end of the bar and nodded. "Looks like you've got a problem."

"Well, how you gonna help me?" Jimmy whined.

"I'm not. She's not doing anything illegal." *Technically,* he added to himself. Her smile and husky voice should be on the books at least as a misdemeanor. And her body would be a felony.

"Aw, come on. This is your fault," Jimmy said.

"My fault," Beau echoed in disbelief, still watching Emily. "This should be good. Somebody needs to tell Hank to wipe the drool off his chin."

"Hank's the worst of the bunch," Jimmy agreed. "But this is all your fault. It's those sisters of yours. They talked to Thelma and persuaded her to influence me to hire Emily."

Beau gave a rough chuckle. "And you're afraid Thelma will stop *influencing* you if you fire Emily. You must have liked the way she used her influence."

Jimmy scowled. "Stop it, Beau. It's not a joking matter when a wife withholds her—" he cleared his throat "—affection. It can be downright painful."

Beau smirked. "You can handle it."

Jimmy sighed and hunkered closer to Beau. "What I need is for someone to take Emily off the market.

Then these dogs would go back to buying beer and leave her alone.''

His bachelor survival instinct rose inside him higher than a killer wave. Beau immediately shook his head. ''No way. Get another sucker. Besides, nobody would believe I'd let a woman get her hooks in me.''

''But you—''

At that moment Hank dropped to his knees in front of Emily and took her hands in his. Emily looked down at him in bemusement as the crowd roared with laughter.

Beau watched Hank's mouth form those timeless suicidal words, ''Marry me.''

''This is pathetic,'' Beau muttered, and noticed that most everyone grew silent in order to hear what Emily would say.

She disengaged her hands and backed away. ''No thank you,'' she said quietly, but firmly. ''I won't marry you.'' Frustration tugged at her face and she raised her voice. ''I'm not getting married. Do you hear me? I'm not getting married. Ever.''

A long silence followed.

Hank's disappointment showed, then another idea must have occurred to him. ''Does that mean you'll consider living in sin?''

During his late-night driving patrol, Beau rounded the turn, and the beam from his headlights skimmed over the vehicle pulled off the road. He slowed. Pine Mountain Lake was off-limits after sundown. It took only a second look for him to ID the car—the only BMW in town.

Beau pulled to a stop and sighed. What was Emily doing here? He checked his watch and got out of his car. It was almost midnight.

She stood a few feet from the moonlit water, her hair catching the reflection of the moon. An ethereal sight, she stared down at something in her hand. She looked lonely. The notion made him uncomfortable, though he wasn't sure why. He cleared his throat. "Emily," he said, keeping his voice low so he wouldn't startle her.

"Hello, Sheriff Ramsey," she said without turning her head.

He came to a stop beside her. "How did you know it was me?"

"The squad car."

She was looking at her engagement ring, Beau noted. "Did you see the No Trespassing After Dark sign?"

"Yes," she said, closing her fingers around the ring and shaking it as if it were dice.

"Then you know you're not supposed to be here."

Her face went solemn for a moment, then seemed to clear. She turned to him. "I guess that means I'm breaking the law. What are you going to do about it?" she asked with an odd mix of politeness and defiance, then strolled closer to the water.

Beau stifled a sigh and followed. He could opt for a hard-nosed approach, but he knew what kind of effect his sisters could have on a person. "Are my sisters driving you nuts yet?"

"Not really," she said. "But sometimes it's difficult to think with people around, even if they're kind.

And your sisters are very kind.'' She glanced at him. ''I like it here at night. You should change the law.''

Beau bit back a wry grin. ''You've got me confused with the town council. I don't make the rules. I just try to keep the peace.''

''I bet you could get them to change it.''

He glanced at her curiously. She was a strange bird. ''Why would I want to do that?''

''Because it's nice here at night. Quiet and peaceful. You can almost hear yourself think.''

''The teenagers used to go parking here. The parents got bent out of shape.''

''Where do they go now?''

''Dirt road behind the Massenberg farm.''

She nodded, but didn't say anything.

Beau studied her. Again she reminded him of a woman who had been pushed just a little too far. Thank God, she didn't look like she was going to cry, but the anger and apathy glinting in her eyes made him uneasy. Through personal experience, he'd learned anger and apathy could be a damn dangerous combination.

''What's on your mind, Emily?'' he asked, struggling with his oath to stay away from damsels in distress.

She sighed and shook the ring in her hand again. ''I'm trying to decide what to do with this ring. Since I technically broke the engagement, I suppose proper etiquette would indicate that I should return it.'' Proper etiquette had been the guiding force in her life since she could remember.

He shoved his hands in his pockets. "Do you think you earned it?"

She looked at him. "The ring? Earned the ring?" Emily frowned as she considered that. She wondered why it was easier to talk in the dark sometimes. "Do you mean sexually?" she asked.

He stepped closer, and his warmth rippled against her like a touch. She shivered, denying the sensation. She felt his intent gaze on her, but it was easier to pretend his dark eyes weren't quite so penetrating under the cover of night.

"It doesn't have to be sexually. You probably shelled out the bucks for the wedding."

Emily felt a familiar sinking sensation in her stomach. "My mother and stepfather did." She had tried to call her mother several days ago to explain, but according to the housekeeper, her mother was *indisposed*.

"Bet you had a good reason for calling it off."

"I didn't really call it off," she said, recalling the way her mouth had refused to promise her undying love to a man who didn't love her.

Beau didn't say anything, and because he didn't prod she felt free to tell him.

Emily opened her hand and looked at the one-carat diamond solitaire. "You know that part of the ceremony where the minister says, 'Do you take this man to be your lawfully wedded husband?' That's when you're supposed to say 'I do.'"

"I guess," he muttered as if he was strictly lukewarm on the subject of marital vows.

"I said, 'I don't believe I will. Thank you very much.'"

He paused, then let out a rough chuckle. "Is that when your mother fainted?"

Emily tried to recall. "No. The minister asked me to repeat myself, so I did. I told Carl to make sure he returned all the gifts, then I left. I think her head hit the pew in front of her when I stepped down from the platform."

He continued to chuckle.

"It wasn't funny," she told him stiffly, but the image of her slack-jawed never-to-be husband had her swallowing her own laughter. "I did give Carl my bouquet. I thought it was appropriate since he—" She broke off when Beau snorted.

"He was probably hoping for more than flowers."

Emily felt the familiar burn of anger run through her. When she'd first learned Carl was in love with another woman, she'd felt hurt, betrayed and angry. "He'd gotten that the week before with his girlfriend in South America."

She took a deep breath, hoping the good sheriff wouldn't give her some platitude about how it was better to find out before the wedding than after. It might be true, but she still wasn't in the mood to hear it. She glanced down at the ring, tossed it slightly above her hand, then caught it. "So now I need to decide what to do with the ring. I could return it."

"Nah. I'd say you've earned it."

Emily felt her heart lighten. She tossed the ring up again. "I could have it remounted into a necklace."

"Be careful how far you throw that. It's dark out here."

"I could give it away," she continued, tossing it higher as if she hadn't heard him.

"Emily—"

"I could throw it in the lake." The appalling notion delighted her. She tossed the ring still higher. "Imagine that. Sensible Emily St. Clair throwing her engagement ring into the—"

Beau's hand stretched in front of her and he caught the ring. "Did you fall into the tequila again? Let me smell your breath."

"Give me the ring," she said, extending her hand.

"Not until you prove you're sane."

Anger licked through her. "Is it part of your job description to determine sanity?"

"In this county?" he asked. "Yes."

"I'm perfectly sober," she told him and stretched on tiptoe so he could smell her. "I told you. Wintergreen," she murmured, describing the flavor of the mint she'd eaten.

He slid his hand around her back to steady her, and her heart started to pound against her rib cage. She was struck again by his size, his broad shoulders that looked as if he could carry whatever was thrown at him. The combination of his aftershave and elusive masculine scent wrapped around her. She instinctively inhaled deeply and felt a disconcerting surge of dizziness.

"Exhale," he muttered, dipping his head.

She breathed in again. "What?"

"Breathe out."

Feeling confused and ridiculous, she pursed her lips and blew in his face. She stared at his mouth, inches from hers, for a long moment. *Did it feel as hard as it looked?* She shook her head. "I told you," she said breathlessly. "Wintergreen. Now give me the ring."

He paused and studied her, his hand still wrapped around her. "What are you going to do with it?"

She wiggled slightly, but she might as well have been trying to move a boulder. "I'm considering my options."

"I'm not letting you throw it into the lake."

"I wasn't aware there was a law preventing me from throwing my ring in the lake," she told him, wishing he weren't so close, wishing she was having an easier time breathing.

"There is tonight," he said.

Emily reached for his hand, but he ducked it behind his back. "I don't make a habit of discussing a person's size, but you should know that your body could intimidate a smaller person."

His dark gaze caught hers and his lips tilted slightly. "Is that what you're feeling, Emily? Intimidated?"

Frustrated. Annoyed. Frustratingly, annoyingly attracted. *Where had that thought come from?*

"Give me my ring. I can throw it in the *sewer* if that's what I want to do." She widened her eyes at the shocking idea. She almost couldn't believe she'd thought of it. *"The sewer,"* she whispered. "That's even better than the lake."

Beau stared at her and swore under his breath. "Lady, you are not playing with a full deck."

"No one has ever called me crazy," Emily told him

solemnly. "I've been described as sensible and dependable. I've always saved for a rainy day, invested in a conservative mutual fund, voted Republican and was engaged to a doctor. I've never gotten a speeding ticket, never gone parking at a lake or behind anybody's farm, never been drunk until last week."

She pursed her lips, silent for a moment. She looked as if she were considering the direction her life had taken. A wildness glinted in her eyes. "Give me the ring."

Beau swore again. No skin off his back, he tried to tell himself. He should just let the crazy lady toss her ring into the lake, but he knew she would regret it later. Lowering his head so that she was forced to look into his eyes, he quickly stuffed the ring in his pocket and took her shoulders in his hands. "What is it gonna take to get your attention?"

Her eyes met his, dropped to his mouth, then returned to lock with his. He watched her lips part slightly and felt a jolt in his gut.

"I, uh—" she said in a husky voice and swallowed "—think you've got my attention," she finished in a whisper.

Her eyelids fluttered and he breathed in her soft, floral scent. "Then you know you can't throw a diamond ring in the lake," he said, sticking to the original issue, though a rush of sexual curiosity was flooding his veins.

"I can't?" she echoed.

"You can't," he said, fighting a compelling urge to kiss her. "Hock it and buy something you want."

"Like what?"

He shrugged, still distracted by her mouth. "I don't know. Women always want things." He was *not* going to kiss her.

"Hmmm," she said.

The sound she made affected him like an intimate caress. Beau bit back a groan and cleared his throat. "A shopping spree, some kind of trinket, a trip."

Beau watched in disbelief as she lifted her face closer to his. Inch by incredible inch, Emily closed the distance between them and her lips meshed with his.

It was the barest brushing of lips, yet he would have sworn a spark of static electricity flickered between them. Wide-eyed, Emily immediately backed away. She looked as surprised at her overture as Beau was.

Irritated with his exaggerated arousal, Beau dropped his hands from her shoulders. "Why in hell did you do that?"

"I'm sorry," she said quickly. "It was incredibly forward, wasn't it? I've never done it before, never really initiated kissing a man, that is. But you were so close and I kept staring at your mouth. I wondered if it was—" She broke off, clearly struggling for composure.

"You wondered what?"

She folded her hands. "I wondered if your mouth was hard. Or not." Her gaze slid self-consciously from his. "Again, I apologize. Could I please have my ring? I'd like to go home now."

Beau switched gears again, trying to keep up with her. He would think about that kiss later, about how warm and soft her mouth had felt, about how he'd wanted to taste her, about how he'd wanted to feel her body pressed against his. He pulled the ring from his pocket and narrowed his eyes. "Are you going to throw it in the lake?"

She hesitated. "Not tonight."

He shook his head and gave it to her. "If you get the urge to toss that ring, call me first. Okay?"

She closed her hand around the ring and began backing away. "I'll certainly give that some thought. Good night, Sheriff."

Then Beau watched as she practically ran to her car. Now that was one weird cookie, he thought.

So why were his lips still burning?

Emily closed the guest bedroom door behind her and took a long careful breath.

She was going insane.

Glancing down at the ring in her hand, she still wished she'd thrown it into the lake. She supposed flushing it down the toilet would accomplish the same task, but her creative nature liked the lake idea better. She liked the image of sending Carl for a long walk on a short pier.

It wasn't that she'd been desperately in love with Carl, but she had made plans. She'd set her mind and will to the life they would share together. If her heart hadn't exactly followed, well, she hadn't focused on that.

She thought now as she stared at the ring, perhaps she should have.

Emily was beginning to think she might need to start listening to her heart and not just her head. It was a different approach for her, and she wasn't exactly sure *how* to do it.

She suspected kissing the sheriff just because she was fascinated by his mouth wasn't a great first step. Groaning in embarrassment, she covered her eyes. It was obvious Beau Ramsey not only didn't approve of her, he didn't like her. He thought she was a frivolous mental lightweight. Which wasn't true! she thought in frustration.

Memories of the past ten years of her life rolled through her head. Almost every decision she'd made, from her clothes, to her education, to her fiancé, had been made because it was expected of her.

She was expected to be sensible and accommodating. She was the one everyone depended on to just go along with what was best.

Impatience flashed through her. The feeling was rising inside her more and more frequently. She'd had enough of doing what everyone else thought she should do. She'd done it so much she wasn't completely sure what she herself wanted anymore.

Enough.

It was time to cut Emily loose and find out what Emily really wanted in life. Ruxton was the perfect place. Nobody knew her, so she didn't have to be totally sensible. She could even go a little wild.

Three

―――

"**B**eau's not all bad," Rosemary said, as she gave her four-year-old daughter a graham cracker and quick kiss. "He'd make a wonderful father and a nice husband."

Caroline sipped her coffee and rolled her eyes at her sister's remark. "Are you confused? Beau would make a nice husband if he wanted to get married, Rosemary."

"You're being too hard on him. He just hasn't found the right woman, yet."

"He prefers floozies," Caroline said. "That Donna woman he's seeing now has been around the block more than once."

"Donna?" Emily prompted when she could get a word in edgewise. Beau's three sisters got together for coffee at least once a week, and they had insisted she join them. She hadn't expected them to be so free with their discussion about Beau, but she was curious about him. Too curious, she thought, recalling the way she'd kissed him last night. She gave herself a hard shake.

Knowledge was power, she told herself. The more she knew about Beau, the less curious she would be. When no one responded to her, she repeated herself. "Donna?"

Valene nodded. "Donna is his current..." Her face creased as she searched for the appropriate word.

"Lady friend," Rosemary offered uncertainly, as she sent her daughter into the next room to play.

Caroline snorted. "Try occasional bedmate."

Valene frowned at her sister. "There are children within hearing distance."

"Excuse me. How would you describe her?"

"I'm not sure I would call her a true lady. Their relationship is difficult to categorize."

Caroline turned to Emily. "Donna and Beau don't have a relationship. They have an arrangement. A no-commitment, no-strings arrangement."

"So, they're lovers," Emily concluded, and felt her curiosity grow. She'd never been anyone's *lover*. She didn't think any man had ever felt that passionate about her, and she'd never felt that kind of passion for any man. Even for the man she had planned to marry. Emily suppressed a wince at that thought.

All three sisters looked at her in shock.

Valene shook her head. "I'm not sure Beau uses the *L* word."

"Or the *M* word," Caroline added.

"Love and marriage?" Emily asked, and watched

Caroline nod. "It sounds as if he may have a limited vocabulary."

Valene laughed. "I think I like that assessment best," she said, then refilled Emily's coffee cup. "The truth is that several years ago Beau was head over heels with a debutante who lived in the next county. She played with him and led him on, then married a lawyer from Raleigh. Soon after that, Beau left Ruxton for a long time."

Rosemary sighed. "He's never been the same. I think, deep down, he's lonely."

Emily wondered about that. Beau seemed like a completely self-contained man, under control. He was the kind who called the shots. "It's hard for me to imagine him falling that hard for a woman."

Caroline nodded. "It was a long time ago. The way he protects his bachelorhood now you'd think he was guarding Fort Knox. But he still has a man's normal drive."

"Caroline," Valene said, "it's not appropriate to discuss Beau's drive."

"I'm only explaining for Emily," she retorted. "It's a sad waste of masculinity. Beau is all man. Yes, and women seem to sense it. They're always throwing themselves at him and making fools of themselves."

Emily's stomach sank. "Throwing themselves at him," she repeated.

"Bringing him meals," Rosemary said.

"Offering to clean his house," Valene offered.

Emily didn't know whether to feel relieved or not. At least she hadn't cooked for him or offered to clean his house.

"Of course, there are others who try a more physical approach." Caroline lowered her voice. "You know how some women rub up against men like cats in heat. I know of one who was even bold enough to kiss him."

Emily nearly scalded her tongue with her coffee. She winced.

"Caroline," Valene said in a warning voice, then turned to Emily with a gentle smile. "Don't worry. He stays away from the good women. You won't have a bit of trouble with him."

From the screen door of her rented home, Emily saw the mattress first, then the man's boots. "Tom?" she said, expecting Rosemary's husband.

"No," the distinctive baritone voice behind the mattress said.

Emily grimaced. "Sheriff Ramsey," she managed to say, feeling a strange shimmy inside her. "How kind of you. Rosemary told me she would send Tom with the bed."

"He was busy. You gonna hold that door open?"

"Of course." Emily opened the door and moved to the side.

"Which room?"

"Upstairs at the end of the hall."

He grunted. "Figures."

"I can help—"

"Please don't."

Emily watched him haul the mattress upstairs, and despite his sour attitude, she couldn't help noticing what a nice rear end the good sheriff had. She blinked at her observation and shook her head. The last time she'd gotten fixated on part of Beau Ramsey's anatomy, she'd kissed him. What was she going to do this time? Pat him or pinch him? Emily bit back a groan.

He brought up the box spring and frame, and she followed with the headboard. It took just a few minutes to put it all together. Emily stared at the bed and felt a rush of excitement.

"You look like you've got plans for this bed," Beau said dryly.

"I do," she said brightly as she reached for the shopping bag of new linens. "I bought two sets of sheets and a comforter. It's hard to believe, but this will be the first time I've lived alone," she confessed.

He raised his eyebrows. "Is that so?"

She wondered why she felt uneasy under his intense gaze. Other men had looked at her before, and it hadn't affected her at all. She tore the plastic wrap off one set of linens and filled the silence. "Yes, my mother was a little overprotective. She was always afraid some hoodlum on a motorcycle would seduce me away from what she called 'a better life.'" Emily laughed. "Now that I've lived the better life, I'm wondering…"

Beau narrowed his eyes slightly. "You're thinking about finding a hoodlum on a motorcycle to seduce you."

She looked at him in surprise. "No. Actually I was wondering what it would be like to *be* a hoodlum on a motorcycle."

Beau pictured Emily decked out in leather on a Harley-Davidson, her blond hair flying, her soft smile slip-

ping into a bad-girl grin, and felt a jolt to his system.
Before everything was said and done, he suspected he
was going to have to lock this woman up. He cleared
his throat. "Let me help you get these on the bed."

"It's not necessary" she said, tossing the bottom
sheet over the bed. "You've already done enough."

"No big deal." He helped make the bed in sheets
with tiny pink rosebuds. He chuckled to himself. Emily might say motorcycles, but she was still a flowers
and lace kind of woman. Beau had learned a long time
ago. It was no use fighting who you were, and though
it wasn't his nature, he felt compelled to remind her
of that fact. "Emily, sometimes a little freedom affects
people like tequila, makes them do things they
wouldn't normally do, things they might regret later."

She smoothed her hands over the sheets and glanced
up at him. "What do you mean?"

He was distracted by the way her hands stroked the
crisp cotton. The movement was sensual, and it made
him wonder how her small feminine hands would feel
on his bare skin, on his chest and abdomen, and lower.
He frowned at the thought and looked away. "I mean,
you've got to be who you are. Take for example these
sheets. Roses. Now why doesn't that surprise me? You
look like a roses, diamonds and champagne kind of
woman."

Emily stopped and stood. "The sheets I choose to
buy have nothing to do with the kind of person I am.
I don't like champagne very much, and I haven't had
much luck with diamonds, so in my case, appearances
must be deceiving."

She had that hint of a wild look in her eyes again.

Beau felt a lick of uneasiness. "You didn't throw away that diamond ring, did you?"

"No. I took your suggestion and pawned it. As a matter of fact, I'm using part of the money to rent this house."

"Great," he said, wondering if he should have told her to toss it. Then maybe she would have left Ruxton behind. "You've decided to stay awhile. You're ready to stay in a town where we get excited about the tractor-pull race on Saturday night?" he asked, reminding her that she might be happier elsewhere.

"Where will it be held?"

He chuckled and shook his head. "I don't think it's your kind of entertainment."

She lifted her chin, tempted to show Mr. Know-it-all the other sheets in the bag, which were *not* covered with roses. "Do you always jump to rash conclusions about newcomers?"

"Rash?" he drawled. "Considering your intoxicated state and your dress the first time we met, I think I've been reasonable."

She felt a pinch of self-consciousness and wished she wasn't blushing. "I would like to believe you could get past that."

He nodded. "A week later I watched a man drop to his knees to propose marriage to you in the bar."

Emily frowned, feeling her cheeks blaze. "I didn't encourage him."

"Soon after that I watched you nearly throw a diamond in the lake." He said it as if he still couldn't believe it.

"And now I suppose you're going to bring up the

fact that I kissed you," she said heatedly, to get it out of the way. "I apologized. I told you—"

He shook his head slowly and looked deliberately at her mouth. "I wasn't going to bring that up." His voice was low, and if she didn't know better, she might think Beau hadn't minded her kissing him nearly as much as she'd first supposed.

Turning away from that insanity, she gave a heavy sigh. "I need a new start. A clean slate with new people and no expectations. You're never going to understand this, but I feel as if I've been living my whole life to meet other people's expectations. Somewhere in all that, I got lost. And I don't want to be lost anymore."

A long silence followed, a silence when she wondered why she'd felt compelled to explain herself to Beau who obviously didn't approve of her.

"What makes you think I wouldn't understand?"

"Oh," she said in frustration, picking up a pillow to fluff it. "You were probably born with enough self-assurance for three people. You know who you are, and if someone doesn't like it, you couldn't care less. You don't have the plague of being a people pleaser."

"I was just plagued by three interfering, busybody sisters," he said in his distinctive, wry voice.

Emily bit her lip to keep from smiling and met his gaze. From her own experience, she'd learned that although Beau's sisters were as kind as the day was long, they could *hover*. "It must have been challenging in high school," she murmured.

"It's challenging *now*. They show up at my house at the crack of dawn, Rosemary straightens everything up so I can't find anything and Valene confiscates my—'' He broke off abruptly as if he changed his mind about revealing more.

It wasn't polite to pry, she thought, and prompted him anyway. ''She confiscates what?''

He met her gaze and reluctantly muttered, ''My cigars.''

''Cigars,'' she echoed. ''I didn't know anyone besides Rodney Dangerfield smoked them anymore.''

''Don't get started on the health risks,'' he growled.

''Oh, I wasn't,'' she said, sinking down on the bed. ''I've always been a little curious about cigars.''

''You want to smoke a cigar?'' he asked in disbelief.

Emily felt her cheeks heat again. ''Not really smoke,'' she murmured, recalling the sensual image she'd once seen in a movie that had stirred her curiosity.

He stepped closer, his large frame pushing into her personal space. Her gaze fell helplessly down from his belt buckle. His jeans might as well have been custom made, the way they skimmed over his muscular thighs and cupped his masculinity.

''Then what?'' he asked.

Dropping her gaze to his boots, Emily shifted on the bed and took a careful breath. ''It's silly. Nothing really.''

''If it's nothing, then why not tell me?'' His husky drawl taunted her.

Rattled, she responded to the challenge. ''I always thought it might be fun to—'' She stopped midsentence, changing her mind.

"Fun to do what?" he prompted as he sat down beside her, using the mild tone he probably used to interrogate suspects.

No way out, she thought, reluctantly meeting his gaze. She finished in a low voice. "Fun to light a man's cigar."

His dark eyes flickered dangerously, but he didn't move closer. "You mean in a restaurant or a bar?"

"Not really," she said, curious about that flicker in his eyes, curious about the sensation in the pit of her stomach. "I mean in bed."

His nostrils flared as he sucked in a deep breath. He leaned over her. "Emily, since you haven't been on your own, I'm gonna give you a little warning. You might not want to tell a man you're curious about lighting his cigar in bed, or he'll expect you to do more than strike a match."

Her chest tightened, and she breathed in his scent. His dark eyes fascinated her. She swallowed. "I haven't told anyone about the cigar thing," she told him. "Besides you're the sheriff and you think I've got as much substance as cotton candy, so you don't really count."

"I don't count," he repeated.

Her stomach flipped again. "You're not attracted to me."

He just stared at her.

"You don't approve of me," she babbled to fill the silence. "You're the sheriff. I can trust you."

"Oh, Emily." Beau swore under his breath and rubbed his face. "I'm sworn to uphold the law, but

I'm no priest." He waited a beat, and his gaze swept over her. "Your body's fair game."

Emily gulped. "Bu-but—but you think I'm a piece of fluff."

He shook his head. "I never said you were a piece of fluff."

"But you think it," she insisted.

"I think," he told her, "you are a woman on the verge of causing a lot of trouble. I'm torn between locking you up or locking up the entire male population of Ruxton. Here's a newsflash, princess, I'm a member of the male population."

"Is this your way of saying you're somewhat attracted to me?"

"It's my way of saying I saw you half-naked that first night, and I haven't forgotten the color of your nipples and the fact that your breasts are larger than they look hiding under your clothes. It's my way of saying I liked what I saw and wouldn't mind seeing you that way again." He leaned closer, but lowered his voice. "It's my way of saying *I count*."

She felt a blast of hot, purely sexual curiosity mixed with a tingle of apprehension, and she didn't have a clue what to do with either feeling. The tension between them was as tight as a steel spring.

"Do you understand what I'm saying?" he asked as he lifted his finger to her chin, then grazed it upward over her mouth.

She could have pulled back, but something inside her wouldn't allow it. Instead, she instinctively parted her lips and he slipped his finger inside her mouth. A sensual invasion. Her heart pounded against her rib cage.

As her gaze locked with his, she flicked her tongue over his skin and tasted him.

He went very still. "You're not listening, Emily. I said I count."

The warning in his eyes, more than his voice, got through to her. She gradually backed away, then looked away from him. "I understand," she managed finally. "You count."

She heard the ragged release of his breath. "Don't forget it," he muttered and stood.

Too restless to remain seated, she stood, too, and tripped over the bag of the other sheets. They slid out of the bag across the floor. Emily winced.

Beau reached down and picked up the sheets from the floor.

Emily felt as if he were looking at her lingerie. She didn't need to see his face to hear the question in his mind. "Just another set of sheets," she said, and pulled them from his hands.

He chuckled, but the sound was strained. "Right. Just another set of sheets." He walked away, and she heard him swear before he muttered, "Black satin."

In the darkness of his den, in his favorite over-stuffed chair, Beau inhaled the fine cigar and waited for the familiar mellow sense of satisfaction. With his black lab lying quietly at his feet, he waited. And waited.

Irritation nicked at him. He set the cigar in the ash-tray and brooded. He'd taken a woman out for the

evening. Donna Grant had given him all the right sig-
nals that she would be willing for him to stay with her
until morning. He and Donna had an arrangement. She
didn't try to pin him down, he didn't make promises
he wouldn't keep, and they got along because they
could bring each other satisfaction without a lot of
extra baggage.

Beau could have been in Donna's bed at this very
minute, but his mind was filled with the image of another woman and another bed. A woman with silky
blond hair, a quick, honest smile and blue eyes that
changed like the weather. It was easy for him to vi-
sualize her wrapped in nothing but a black satin sheet.
Easy for him to imagine the creamy softness of her
throat, the upper curve of her breasts and the pebbled
hardness of her small rosy nipples.

His body swelled in response. Still irritated, Beau
picked up the cigar and drew on it again. He narrowed
his eyes. She was curious about him. He'd seen the
sexual curiosity in her gaze, the drive to explore his
desire and her own. She had an innocent look to her.
For a crazy moment, he wondered if she was a virgin.

He shook off that notion. Women, no, make that
girls, shed their virginity at a younger age nowadays.
She was just inexperienced. With her wedding fiasco
still fresh in her mind, she was also vulnerable. She
was probably convinced she wasn't the marrying kind,
and under the right conditions, could be coaxed into
an affair to soothe her wounded feminine ego.

Beau flicked his ashes into the ashtray and considered the situation from a different angle. If he was a
nice guy, he would leave her alone. He would give

her a wide berth and let someone else console Emily. If he followed his instincts, he would stay the hell away from her. She was like a champagne bottle that had been shaken up. When her cork popped, all hell was going to break loose.

The image of her wrapped in a black satin sheet, however, was like an intimate stroke that teased and promised satisfaction. And Beau was suffering from a gnawing sense of dissatisfaction. He wondered how she would taste. He wondered how her eyes would change when he touched her. He wondered what husky words of need she would whisper.

He wondered a helluva lot about Miss Emily. If he was a nice guy, though, he would leave her alone. Beau had never considered himself a nice guy. He was a wolf. There was still the matter of his instincts, however. He rarely strayed from the practice of following his instincts, because on the few occasions he had, he'd gotten burned. Unfortunately, with the image of Emily singeing his mind, he was already burning up and he hadn't done a thing.

Emily didn't make it to the tractor pull, but she did take in the Ruxton Flea Market on Saturday morning. Held in the parking lot of the big Methodist church on Main Street, the flea market exhibited a carnival atmosphere. Aside from a myriad of vendors, a group of musicians played bluegrass, a woman gave Tarot card readings and another woman, dressed as a clown, twisted balloons into animals and crazy hats.

She was surprised to see Beau strolling among the vendors. He nodded slowly upon seeing her and moved toward her. She watched his face and would have sworn she'd seen something primitive and predatory flash across his features, but then he gave her that cocky half grin. "Missed you at the festivities last night," he said.

"I'm sure you did," she said, full of skepticism. "I wouldn't have thought this would be your choice of venue for a Saturday morning."

He walked alongside her. "We had a little problem with homemade liquor last month."

"Oh," Emily said, and lowered her voice. "Moonshine. Did you have to make a raid?"

"I confiscated it," he said with a too-straight face.

Emily studied him carefully. "Did you taste any of it?"

"Only to validate the fact that it hadn't been approved by the ABC. We don't have a lab available for small cases."

She laughed despite herself. "How much did you drink for this validation?"

"Not much," he admitted. "I needed a fire extinguisher after one gulp."

She stepped up to the pretzel vendor. "Would you like one?" she asked Beau.

He looked surprised. "Yeah."

She handed him the warm, salty pretzel and took a bite of her own. "I'm still surprised you didn't find someone else for this detail. Shopping," she said with a smile.

"My part-time deputy's on vacation. It's not so bad. Pretty blondes buy me pretzels. Changed your sheets yet?" he asked slyly.

She willed her cheeks not to heat. "I usually change them once a week. I've never slept on satin, so it'll be a new experience." *Give it back to him,* she told herself. "Have you?"

He gave her a double take. "Have I what?"

"Ever slept on satin sheets?" she asked, and watched a fleeting uneasiness cross the sheriff's face. Something about that expression gave her a strange sense of power.

He paused, his uneasiness short-lived. "No," he said, taunting her with his devil dark eyes. "Care to give me a new experience?" His voice was as slick as her satin sheets.

Emily felt herself getting in over her head. She took a quick breath. "I—uh—" She glanced around wildly. "Ever had a balloon hat before?"

"No, but—"

Emily gave the clown the high sign before Beau could finish, and within a minute, she placed the balloon Indian hat in his hand with a smile. "There. Now you can't say I've never given you a new experience."

Beau looked at the balloon. "You're not as fluffy as I thought."

Emily gave a low laugh. "You're not quite as fast as I thought."

His eyes instantly proved her a liar, moving over her body at Mach speed. "I was a rodeo rider, princess. You'd be surprised what I can do in eight seconds."

A rodeo rider? A cowboy? She was so surprised that she didn't immediately respond. The moment passed, and a child's wail cut through the happy sounds of the crowd.

Beau glanced away from her and moved toward the wailing. Emily instinctively followed behind him. At the end of the row of vendors stood a little girl, crying at the top of her lungs. Tears stained her cheeks, and the look of fear on her face grabbed at Emily's heart.

Emily watched Beau kneel down in front of her and speak quietly. The child's eyes rounded with even more fear until he offered the balloon hat. The moppet eyed him suspiciously, but clenched the balloon in her hand. "I can't find my mama."

"Well, we should be able to fix that. Can you tell me your name?"

"Hil'ry." She backed away slightly.

Beau nodded. "And your mother's name."

Hilary frowned at him. "Regina," she whispered.

"And your last name?" Beau prompted.

"I don't want you. I want my mama." She began to cry again.

The sound tore at Emily. She didn't want to intrude, but didn't think she would hurt the situation any. Stepping closer to the little girl, she pulled a generous piece off her pretzel. "Would you like a bite of my pretzel until your mother gets here?"

Hilary scrutinized Emily and the pretzel, then sniffed and wiped her nose with the back of her hand. "Yes, ma'am. Thank you."

Within a couple of minutes, Hilary scarfed down the rest of Emily's pretzel and had taken residence in her lap. The experience bemused Emily because she'd never considered herself particularly adept with children, even when she'd been one. The slight weight of Hilary in her lap, the sunshine scent of her hair and the simplicity of a shared treat tugged at her. There was an indescribable pleasure having a child befriend you even if it was by way of a bribe.

"See if you can get her last name out of her," Beau muttered, as he brought another pretzel.

Emily nodded. "Hilary's a nice name. What's your last name?"

"Bell," she said around a bite of pretzel. She tossed Beau another scowling glance.

Emily laughed. "Is this your first experience with a female who refused to be charmed?"

He shot her an aren't-we-clever look and bent next to Emily's ear. The sensation gave her such a rush she almost didn't hear him. "Get her to talk about her mother. I've asked around and nobody here knows who she is."

"Hilary, where did you last see your mother?"

"She was playing bingo in the church, and I wanted to look at the clown, so I went to the window and watched. And then I kinda went out the door. For just a minute!" she insisted desperately, her face crumpling. "I went back and she was gone."

Emily gave her a comforting squeeze. "I bet that felt scary."

"Yeah," Hilary said in a quavery voice so quiet Emily almost couldn't hear it. "Can you make that man go away?"

"Why? He's the sheriff. He's here to help you."

Hilary looked unconvinced. "Does he hit? My daddy's big like him, and he hits."

It was a hot, summer day, but Emily felt as if someone had just injected ice water in her veins. She took
a deep breath and searched for her composure; at the
same time her gaze met Beau's. "No, sweetheart. The
sheriff doesn't hit."

She watched something happen in Beau Ramsey's
eyes—anger, rare, righteous anger; and compassion,
strong and powerful. And that combination rocked her
world.

Four

Beau's tension surrounded him like a force field. Within minutes he'd located Regina Bell and had a quiet talk with her while Emily entertained Hilary. Regina had been frantically searching for Hilary inside the church. Regina and Hilary left with Emily promising to visit her new little friend again soon.

The swap meet began to disassemble—a morning crowd of people who obviously had other things to do in the afternoon. From a few feet away, Emily sensed the strength of Beau's disquiet as she watched him making some notes as he sat in the squad car. Her ability to feel his feelings disturbed her. While she often read other people's emotions accurately, she also could usually distance herself. This time she couldn't, and she wasn't sure why.

She took a couple of steps closer to Beau and

crossed her arms over her chest. *What to say,* she wondered, yet knew she had to say something. "No white lightning today," she murmured.

He glanced at her, the anger and compassion still glowing from his eyes. "White lightning's a helluva lot easier to deal with."

"She wouldn't press charges?"

"No." He rose from the car as if he couldn't bear to sit any longer. "She said he's not living with them anymore. She just wants to put it in the past."

"And you're concerned it won't stay in the past," Emily continued.

He narrowed his eyes. "She's serving him with divorce papers, and he's got a nasty temper."

Emily felt a chill. "The story's all too common, isn't it?"

He slammed his car door. "Not in Ruxton, dammit. Not in my town."

His anger washed over her, surprising her into momentary silence. "What did you do?" she asked when she found her voice.

"I told her to call me if she changed her mind or if her ex comes calling." He shook his head. "She won't."

It made no sense to her, but she wanted him to feel better. "You did what you could."

"It's not enough."

Her immediate thought was bold, and she almost didn't say it, but she decided to go with her heart and not her head for a change. "Do I hear the beginning of a superhero complex?"

He swiveled to stare at her.

Her courage bolstered by his response, she walked closer. "Do you have secret powers to make sure Ruxton is a perfect place?"

"What's your point?"

"My point is that you might have a lot of influence, but you're dealing with humans. And humans aren't perfect. It's great that you care so much, but you'll never make Ruxton perfect."

"I didn't say perfect," he told her.

"The domestic disputes get to you, though, don't they?"

He shrugged. "A little." He sighed. "Okay, a lot. When they won't press charges, my hands are tied."

"But you leave the door open?"

"Yeah," he muttered.

"And you still care?"

"Yeah."

"Then I'd say the community of Ruxton is very lucky to have you." She smiled. "Even if you don't wear a superhero uniform under your clothes."

He shot her a disgruntled look, but she felt his mood rise, and strangely enough, she was pleased.

His gaze trapped hers. "Trying to cheer up the sheriff?"

Her cheeks heated. She should have known he would catch her. "Would a pretzel help?"

He flicked his gaze down her body again, making her wonder if he indeed did have superpowers from the heat he generated inside her. "Black satin sheets would help," he said, in a low silky voice.

Her breath stopped somewhere between her throat and her chest. "Your bed is larger than mine," she managed to say, remembering the fateful morning she'd awakened in his big bed. "So my sheets wouldn't fit your bed."

He moved closer to her, his gaze still holding her tight with nerves and anticipation. "You don't have to make the bed with them, Emily. You can just wear them." He paused a half beat. "For a while."

Taking a step backward, she gulped. "Black satin would be too hot for summer."

He matched her step with a cocky, coaxing grin and moved closer again. "You wouldn't have to wear it very long," he promised, then put his index finger over her lips when she opened her mouth. "You've got some very nice excuses, Miss Emily. I've got an answer for all of them."

He would, she thought, and knew he was waiting to bait her while she tried another polite way to wriggle out of this dilemma. She hated the idea of letting him win this little battle of wit and seduction. A series of platitudes about pride and the uselessness of one-upmanship ran through her mind.

Emily paused. *Screw the platitudes.*

"You might have some of the answers," she told him in a voice she tried to make just as silky as his. "But you don't have all of them. Try this one on for size, Sheriff Ramsey." She hitched her chin and met his gaze boldly. "No."

She grinned, immensely pleased with herself. She'd just faced down the sexiest man she'd ever met, and she hadn't even stuttered. "But if you change your mind about the pretzel, let me know. Bye, now."

Then Emily broke another one of the rules for etiquette and left before Beau had a chance to respond.

Beau flipped on the lights in his office, set his cup of fast-food coffee on the corner of his desk and greeted the computer by the obscenity he'd named it. Then he grabbed the sheaf of papers from the fax machine.

Reading the top sheet, he grabbed the coffee maker's glass pot, gave it a quick rinse in the bathroom sink and filled it with water, then added a new filter and coffee, and poured the water.

It was Monday morning. There was a boatload of paperwork from the state and county, and if he was going to separate the wheat from the chaff, he needed his caffeine system running smoothly.

There were a few things Beau didn't like about being the chief lawman of the township of Ruxton. The first was the paperwork. It amazed him how the tentacles of bureaucracy could find their way all the way to such a small town.

The second was that damn computer.

Due to his extensive futile experience with the machine, when he said computer, the word *damn* was always attached. The county had sent it to him several months ago, so he'd glanced through the instruction booklets and given it a whirl. It was the most frustrating three days of his life. He'd been thrown from wild bulls more amenable than the blasted machine.

The damn computer, Beau concluded, was a female. She did, however, come with one handy feature. An On-Off switch. Beau derived a great deal of pleasure in turning her off. But that was the only thing he really knew to do with her.

For the next thirty minutes, he filtered through the paperwork, making a small pile for the useful information, another pile for his part-time help to file and ditching the rest.

He was pouring his third cup of coffee when he heard someone step into the outer office. Poking his head through the door, he did a double take when he saw Emily St. Clair meet his gaze. She'd practically run away from him on Saturday. At the moment she looked as if she was struggling unsuccessfully for nonchalance.

"Emily," he said with a nod, and allowed his gaze to drift over her. Her hair was pulled back in a ponytail low on the nape of her neck, and she wore a conservative skirt and white blouse combination. It was both a blessing and a crime, he thought, how her clothes concealed the curves of her body.

"I'm here to set up your computer," she told him.

That stopped his perusal. He glanced back at her face. "My computer?"

"Yes. I've been hired as a temp to get your computer running."

"You?" he said, incredulous. "But you've got a degree in fine art."

The slightest spark of impatience flashed through her eyes before her mouth tilted in amusement. "Yes, but my minor was in computer science. Where's your hardware?"

When he recovered from his shock, Beau almost told her exactly where his personal hardware was, but he bit his tongue, torn between disgust and wry humor. He'd clearly underestimated Emily. In more ways than one, he thought, recalling the satin sheets. "C'mon back," he muttered, and turned around. "She's in the corner of my office."

"She?" Emily echoed.

"Yeah." Beau chuckled under his breath. "I've got a couple of names for her. The latest is PMS."

Emily met his gaze as he glanced over his shoulder, then shook her head. "I would have expected something more original from you. Men are forever using PMS as an explanation for why they don't understand women."

"We like having a label for it, but everyone in this office has taken a whack at her," he explained, and handed Emily the instruction books.

She glanced at them, then blew the dust off the top one. She lifted her eyebrows in mock sympathy. "Your Achilles' heel?"

"You're enjoying this," he said.

Her eyelashes fluttered downward. "Just a little. It's nice to know that even Ruxton's superhero has a weakness."

When Beau looked at Emily, he was entirely too aware of his weakness, but he kept that information to himself. She made him aware of needs long denied. Needs more than physical. "How long are you supposed to be here?"

"As long as it takes to get you operational, then train everyone who works with the computer."

Beau hid his grin. "That long, huh?"

Frowning, she took a seat in front of the computer. "Shouldn't be more than a week."

Beau thought of his part-time help, old Mrs. Bing, who was even less inclined toward computer matters than he. Then there was his deputy. He coughed. "I'll let you get to work."

By lunchtime, Emily was eyeing the weapons in the office. She'd never seen such a mess in her life. Missing files, files in the wrong places: the computer needed therapy. Beau mentioned something about lunch, but she thanked him and shook her head. She was determined to make progress.

Sometime in the afternoon a sandwich appeared beside her. She absently ate it. Later, she'd rolled up her sleeves and discarded her shoes. Her biggest distraction was Beau. She would have worked far more effectively if she hadn't been so aware of him. When he talked on the phone, his low voice seemed to stroke her skin, and his scent seeped into her pores. When he walked in or out of the small room, she had to force herself not to watch the way he moved—a purely masculine stride that was just this side of cocky, but over-the-edge sexy.

Every now and then she felt his gaze on her. The knowledge made her feel hot and achy. Her heart tripped over itself, and she shifted in her seat.

With one glance, he upset her equilibrium.

She hated it.

And liked it.

At the moment she had a reprieve from Beau since he was out of the office. Taking a deep breath, she leaned back in her chair and closed her eyes. Her wrist ached a little from her nonstop disagreement with the computer. She absently rubbed it.

She caught his scent and heard his boots scrape on the floor before she saw him.

"Falling asleep on the job already?" he asked, then glanced at the clock on his desk. "It's past quitting time."

"I know," she murmured, sitting up and turning off the computer. "I had just hoped to get further today."

He nodded and pulled up a chair beside her. "You were rubbing your wrist when I came in."

Emily lifted her right hand. "It's nothing, really. Just overworked it a little today. I—"

He took her wrist in his big hand and gently massaged. The action stole her words and jammed her mind for a full minute. His hand was big and tanned against her smaller fair wrist. The sight of his fingers on her was sensually evocative.

A protest formed in her throat, but his gentleness killed it. She wouldn't have expected him to be so gentle. His callused thumb massaged a sore joint, and she felt her muscles relax. Even her neck muscles loosened. She sighed.

"Carpal tunnel?" he asked in a low voice.

She shook her head. "No. I just overwork it every now and then."

He stretched her fingers and rested her hand on his knee while he rubbed her palm. She bit back a moan and took a deep breath. "I wouldn't have thought giving a hand massage would be one of your talents."

Tossing her a wicked glance, he lightly skimmed

his index finger along the inside of her fingers. The move was provocative. "I have several talents you've never seen me exhibit."

Emily's heart bumped inside her chest. She wondered why she felt as if he was doing something intimate, something sexual to her, when he was merely rubbing her hand. But the strength and warmth of his knee on the underside of her hand, and his fingers alternately massaging and caressing her palm made her conscious of him all over her body. He lightly traced the length of her fingers, and she was amazed to feel warmth suffuse her skin. Her stomach tightened and her breasts ached.

He twined his fingers through hers. "You've got pretty hands."

Emily stared at their joined hands and felt her stomach dip. She'd never thought of her hands as pretty. "Yours are big," she said quietly, wondering how those big, gentle hands would feel all over her body. Wondering, but knowing she wouldn't find out.

Then he shocked her again by lifting her hand to his mouth. His lips were just as she'd remembered, firm but tender.

"Soft," he said, and when she was sure he couldn't surprise her again, he flicked his tongue over her skin. "And sweet."

Emily shuddered. *Where was her mind?* Sanity came screaming to her rescue, and she pulled her limp hand from his. If a hand could protest, hers would have. It was almost as if he'd made love to her fingers and they couldn't seem to function. She cleared her throat. "Uh, thank you. It's uh—much better. You're very good," she managed.

Beau gave a ghost of a grin. "My pleasure."

Emily stood and turned away from him, discreetly fanning herself. She searched wildly for a change of subject. "You mentioned something about being on the rodeo circuit for a while. Do you miss it?"

She felt him stand behind her. "I was on the circuit for seven years and came back to Ruxton after the mayor tracked me down and told me I'd been appointed sheriff. I'd won a few titles, busted everything that could be busted twice, and was tired of traveling."

She stepped slightly away, but turned to face him. "Do you ever miss it?"

"Not much," he muttered. "It wasn't glamorous."

"You rode horses or cows?"

"Mostly horses. I gave up on the bulls," he said, his dark eyes amused, yet somehow sexy. "I never rode any Jersey dairy cattle."

Emily remembered her frequently denied requests for horseback riding lessons. "I always wanted to ride," she murmured, then shook her head when she realized she'd said it aloud.

"What did you say?"

She felt self-conscious. "Nothing really. I—"

"Did you say you wanted to ride?"

"It was a long time ago."

"Just answer the question, Emily," he said, and she noticed he was suddenly entirely too close.

She took a deep breath and made herself meet his gaze. "Okay, yes I wanted to learn."

His lips tilted in that kill-the-ladies-and-make-them-love-it grin. "Oh, Emily, it'll be my pleasure to teach you to ride."

"He's big," Emily said as she gazed warily at Beau's horse, Blue.

He heard the tentative note in her voice. "He's a gelding."

She glanced at him, then back to Blue. "So?"

He chuckled. "So his temperament is nice and easy." He tightened the straps of the saddle and added. "Plus he's older. He doesn't mind taking his time."

Blue pawed the ground, and Emily backed away. "Are you sure about that?"

"Yeah." He rose and looked at her. "Why?"

"Well, just because he's old doesn't mean he's good-natured. I've met quite a few cranky older people." As if she didn't want to offend, she rushed to clarify. "Not that they don't have reason for being cranky. I've met some who have arthritis and others with digestion difficulties. Others are cranky because their children don't visit often enough."

She was so earnest, Beau thought. He nodded soberly, chewing the inside of his cheek to keep from laughing so hard he would burst a rib. "Blue only gets rheumatism on bitter cold winter mornings. His digestion system works just fine. Before he was a gelding he sired about twenty foals, and he's delighted they never come to visit."

"Really?" Still pensive, she looked at Blue again.

Beau realized he'd pushed her to do this. It was completely out of character for him. More than one woman had tried to wrangle riding lessons from him, and he'd become quite adept at dodging the rope. Emily, he knew, wasn't trying to rope him. *She* was trying to dodge *him,* and he knew why. He unsettled her. He was impossible for her to ignore. He made her aware of herself, of her sexuality.

He made her sweat.

Beau hid a grin. He liked making Emily sweat.

He should, however, show a little compassion if she was terrified of horses. "Listen, if you don't want to ride, you don't have to."

Emily swallowed and looked as if she were reaching deep for her fortitude. She shook her head. "No. I want to ride," she told him, as if she were reminding herself. "This is the perfect time for me to do all the things I've wanted to do, but haven't."

Beau could have recommended some other activities to try first, but he thought he was going to have to ease her into those. Ease her out of her clothes and into bed. The thought made his body tighten, but he brushed it aside. He'd promised a riding lesson to the lady, and she was going to get it.

"Good," he said. "Let me help you get a leg up. Left foot in the stirrup. You always mount from the left."

Whispering something under her breath, she did as he instructed. Beau allowed her to brace her hand on his shoulder as she swung her shapely rear end into the air. Beau watched the denim stretch taut over her bottom. He could almost imagine what that sweet derriere would look like nude—fair skin, tight muscle, and the kind of curve that could make him moan. He bit his cheek again, but this time he was holding back that moan, not laughter.

On horseback, Emily followed Beau and his mount back to the barn. It was a warm, humid afternoon, but the summer breeze brought blessed relief. She'd enjoyed the ride around Beau's property, and she was delighted with the fact that she hadn't embarrassed herself by falling off the horse. "I still think I could ride a little longer," she told Beau as he dismounted, then removed the saddle and bridle and released his horse into the pasture.

Emily pulled back on the reins slightly and smiled when Blue stopped. "It's almost like brakes," she murmured.

Beau squinted up at her. "With the right horse, it is," he said, and waved her down. "We've been out a couple of hours. You'll be surprised at all the muscles you used. I don't want you too sore."

"Oh, I won't get sore." She carefully swung her right foot over and slid down the side of the horse.

Beau slowed her swift descent with his hands on her waist. She was surprised at how heavy her feet felt when they touched the ground. Her knees felt as if they'd been pried open, and her muscles were completely uncooperative.

Disconcerted, she stared down at her legs and turned toward him. "They feel like lead jelly."

He winced. "That means you'll be sore tomorrow. I shouldn't have kept you out this long the first time."

She looked up at him. "But I loved it."

His gaze meshed with hers and gentled. "I'm glad."

Emily took a careful breath at the glitter in his dark eyes and smelled the earthy scent of horse, hay and man. His body was close, his large hands encircling her waist. His attention was focused on her, making her feel surrounded by him. He jangled her nerve endings and kicked her stable sensibility straight into the pasture.

Emily had always considered herself a quiet person, inside and out. Being close to Beau, however, made her insides feel as noisy as the percussion section in a high school band.

Struggling with a myriad of sensations, she fell back on her upbringing. "Thank you very much for the lesson," she said.

"You're welcome very much." He lifted one of his hands to cup her jaw. "Your skin's a little pink. Sunburn?"

Emily swallowed the knot of tension in her throat. "It shouldn't be, this late in the day."

"Your skin's so fair I bet you burn like crazy in the summertime." Holding her gaze, he rubbed his thumb under her chin.

His touch made her feel languid and disinterested in moving. "I don't usually stay out in the sun very long in the summertime."

"Your skin is so soft here. Makes me wonder what it feels like other places," he muttered, and moved his index finger down her throat.

Her heart jolted, and her stomach twisted with a

painfully sweet combination of apprehension and anticipation.

Still watching her, he slid his finger down her chest, beneath the open collar of her white cotton shirt, over the upper swell of her breast.

Her breath stopped, and though she knew he would allow her to step away, all she could do was stare into his dark, sensual eyes and wait.

Five

If Emily didn't know better, she would think Beau's eyes were making love to her. But she knew better, a small voice inside her whispered. She knew better.

When he slid his finger over her nipple, however, she didn't know anything. Feeling an overwhelming surge of arousal, she closed her eyes and took a deep breath. "Oh." Her moan escaped her throat.

"Soft and hard," Beau murmured. "Your breast is soft, but the tip is hard." He continued to caress her with just his fingertip.

She should tell him to stop, but she wanted more. He rolled her nipple between his thumb and forefinger. "Touching you isn't enough," he told her and she felt his breath on her face as he lowered his head.

"Touching you makes me want to taste you." His

mouth captured hers and his tongue tangled with hers, tasting and taunting.

Emily felt as if her blood were gasoline and Beau had lit a match and tossed it inside her. She leaned into his hand, pressed her mouth into his and kissed him back.

Beau caught her nonverbal signal and immediately returned it by tugging her shirt open and closing his hand around her breast.

Emily moaned into his mouth and got drunk on his flavor. He tasted warm and seductive. Passionate for *her*. The thought made her weak.

Distantly she felt her shirt slide off one shoulder. It seemed only a second passed and his mouth was closing around her nipple. The sensation was incredible. "Oh, my." He kept on as if he couldn't get enough of her, flicking his tongue, cupping it around the sensitive beaded tip. Emily felt a sharp tug deep in her nether region. Her knees dipped and he caught her against him, reluctantly moving his mouth from her breast.

His heart pounding against hers, he gazed at her with turbulent dark eyes. "I've wanted to do that since the first night I saw you."

One of his hands slid down to her rear end and brought her intimately against him. He was hard and full. She could feel the power of his desire flowing from every pore of his body, moving her, melting her.

He rocked his hardness into the notch of her thighs. With shocking speed, she felt herself grow wet and swollen.

"There's more I want to do with you, Emily," he said low and deep. "A lot more."

Dipping his head, he kissed her again, his tongue sliding in and out of her mouth in an erotic motion that simulated what he clearly wanted to do to her with his whole body.

Emily wanted him. She wanted his mouth and his hands on her. She wanted him deep inside her where no man had ever been. She wanted so much she trembled with it. She wanted everything she'd never had before.

The horse behind her snorted and pawed the ground. Emily distantly noticed the sound.

The horse made another movement, distracting her, and she blinked. The early-evening sunlight was still bright. Her mouth stilled against Beau's. In gradual but swift degrees, Emily realized that given another sixty seconds or so, she would have been in the dirt, tearing off his clothes.

They were both breathing as if they'd run a race. His gaze burned a hole clear to her soul. Somehow he *knew* what was going on inside her.

"I don't know what to say," she whispered.

"We could go inside," he told her.

Emily swallowed hard over the knot of desire in her throat and shook her head. "I—I—I'm not ready."

"For sex," he said.

Agreeing, though her body still called her a liar, she moved her head in a circle. "Right. And you. I'm not ready—for you."

Beau lifted his hand to stroke her hair from her forehead. "It would be good, Emily. Very easy."

Emily gave an involuntary shudder. "Yes, but I was almost getting married three weeks ago." It boggled her mind to recall it.

"Almost," he said pointedly. "I'm not asking for anything permanent. Not marriage," he said. "But we could be good together."

So why not, Emily? She stared at him. Part of her wanted to go inside and let Beau Ramsey make love to her, to make love to him. Part of her wanted to go too far, too fast and do too much. But more than her sensible side was resisting; her heart wasn't ready, either.

Exasperated with her conflicting feelings, she lowered her head and backed away. "I—can't."

"Emily, this is Jenna."

"And Maddie."

The voices of her two longtime friends on the telephone immediately lifted Emily out of her doldrums. Before she picked up the phone, she'd been brooding over Beau Ramsey. She didn't know whether to pat herself on the back for stopping things before they went too far, or kick herself for not giving in to her passions. It didn't help that her posterior was sore from the ride.

"Hi," she said, smiling into the phone. "Both of you at once. Is this a conference call?"

"In a manner of speaking," Jenna said.

"I'm at Jenna's place. I'm talking on the extension," Maddie said. "But what I want to know is why in Hades you're living in a place like Ruxton?"

Emily heard Jenna's sigh. "Maddie, I thought we

agreed we were going to handle this delicately, but since you've asked. Why Ruxton, Em?''

A long silence followed while Emily tried to formulate her answer.

"Emily," Jenna prodded.

"It wasn't exactly planned," Emily said, winding the phone cord around her fingers. She would never confess the truth to anyone but these her closest friends, and she was reluctant to tell them. "I had to use the bathroom and I was thirsty, so I thought Ruxton was as good a place as any to stop."

"But you didn't just stop," Maddie said. "You're *living* there, aren't you?"

Emily glanced around her small kitchen and gave a small laugh. "I guess I am. I'm definitely not coming back to Roanoke."

Jenna cleared her throat. "You mean not right away," she said in her attorney's voice.

"I mean not in this lifetime," Emily said, though she knew her response wasn't the least bit rational.

Another long silence followed.

"I told you, Jenna Jean," Maddie said.

"Jenna," Jenna Jean automatically corrected. She'd been trying to dump what she considered the juvenile addition of her middle name for ten years.

"She's gone straight over the edge."

"She has not. She's just a little rattled," Jenna retorted.

"Off the deep end," Maddie corrected.

"She is not. She's just—"

"Recovering from walking out on her wedding," Emily interjected.

"The wedding of the century," Maddie piped in with an awed tone, making Emily wince. "You've never looked more gorgeous than when you gave your bouquet to Carl."

Emily gave a wry smile. "Thank you. I think."

"We're concerned about you," Jenna said in a quiet voice. "This is out of character for you."

Emily sighed and felt her heart expand at the true care in her friend's voice. "I know it is. When I found out about Carl—"

"And his girlfriend in South America," Maddie added. "I would have kicked him where it counted. You should have taken one of those metal candelabras and bonked him on the head with it."

"Assault," Jenna muttered. "But I must confess I thought you should have set his tux pants on fire."

Emily laughed. "I didn't know what to do, but I couldn't marry him. And I knew it was going to *kill* my mother." Emily began to pace. "I think the wedding was more important to her than it was to me."

"The wedding of the century," Maddie repeated, making Emily's stomach twist in distress again.

"Have you talked to your mother?" Jenna asked.

Emily struggled with guilt and relief. "Her housekeeper, Marie, is her liaison. My mother is *indisposed*, but Marie has had a list of questions each time I called."

"I heard she's gone to one of those exclusive spas," Maddie, who had a good ear for gossip, told her.

"Emily, are you working? Have you met some friends?" Jenna asked.

"Are there any men under the age of eighty?" Maddie asked.

Emily smiled to herself. "Yes, yes and yes." Strange how talking to her longtime friends made her feel stronger. "I'm assessing my life, thinking about what I want instead of what everyone else might want. It'll be easier for me to be different if I'm not in Roanoke."

"Good," Maddie immediately said. "And you're well rid of that prig, Carl Yancey. I always thought he would be rotten in bed, anyway."

Emily sucked in a quick breath and waited for someone to politely fill the silence. No one did. "I wouldn't know," she finally said.

"Oh," Jenna murmured and hesitated a second. "Em, you're not involved with a man already, are you?"

Emily started to move around the kitchen. It gave her the illusion of being a moving target, and Jenna was definitely on the hunt. Jenna Jean Anderson was one of the most disturbingly intuitive people Emily had ever met. "Not really," she hedged. "How's everything at the D.A.'s office?"

"Fine. When you say not really, does that mean you've met someone who appeals to you?"

Emily felt her stomach tense. She really didn't want to discuss this. "I'm not going to do anything about it. I might be doing *some* things I've never done before, but I'm not ready to—"

"Hit the sack," Maddie finished for her and gave a big sigh. "It might be the best thing in the world for you."

"Maddie," Jenna said in an iron tone that intimidated just about everyone. Except Maddie. "We wouldn't be very good friends if we encouraged Emily to do something reckless."

"Okay, okay," Maddie said. "If you decide to hit the sack with this guy, make sure you use contraception," she added, completely missing Jenna's point.

Jenna groaned. "Emily, we care about you. If you need us for anything, anything at all, call. Okay?"

"Thanks, Jen."

"I've got to go," her friend said. "Be careful."

Before Emily could say a word, Maddie piped in. "Here's your chance, Emily. Let her rip. G'night."

Emily said goodbye and hung up, thinking about the divergent advice offered by her two best friends. *Be careful. Let her rip.* It was difficult combining the two.

The next morning Emily walked into the sheriff's office, struggling to shove her edginess way below her outer surface where it wouldn't be seen. She'd always been told to think of Grace Kelly's serene beauty during her times of turmoil. The nervous habits of her youth had been drilled out of her long ago in finishing school. But those same habits, such as biting her lip and fidgeting with her hands, were popping up like pesky, persistent weeds this morning. It didn't help that she knew she wasn't walking normally. Her legs felt stiff and uncooperative from her ride yesterday.

Beau glanced up from drinking his cup of coffee and stopped her with a gaze that slid all the way up and down her body. His gaze lingered at the tops of her thighs, making her struggle with the instinct to rub her legs together to cure the restlessness he caused inside her. Then his dark eyes met hers. "Sore this morning?" he asked in a low, deep voice that made her think of a different, more intimate ride with Beau. His expression said "You could have been with me, sweetheart, and I would have made sure you liked it."

She bit the inside of her upper lip, then realized what she was doing and gritted her teeth together. "A little," she admitted and moved toward the computer. "Thank you for asking. I don't want to interrupt your routine, so I'll go ahead and get to work."

As if he could sense her uneasiness, he grinned slightly and said in a silky tone. "No interruption at all."

She sat down, booted up the computer, narrowed her eyes in deliberation at the screen and told herself to ignore the buzzing sensation inside her. For the next hour and a half, she got a headache trying to get past the Error messages. She repeated commands and backtracked. Despite the fact that her concentration was in the toilet, Emily finally got the programming straightened out. She immediately began sketching out user-friendly instructions for Beau and his office. By the end of the day, she'd obtained a template and mapped out a plan.

"I think this calls for champagne," she murmured to herself, and she leaned back in her chair.

"Good news?" Beau asked.

"Oh, yes," Emily said, the phone ringing at the same moment.

He lifted his hand and picked up the receiver. "Just a minute," he said, and listened to the caller.

Emily watched his face darken and wondered at the cause until he scratched something on a piece of paper and muttered, "Regina Bell".

Emily felt her blood run cold. He asked a few terse questions, then finished his call and headed for the door. Emily stood. "It's Regina. What happened?"

His eyes were as cold and hard as steel. "Her estranged husband decided to pay a call this morning. Her neighbor just took her to the emergency room."

Emily immediately thought of Regina's daughter, the little girl she'd held in her lap. Her heart twisted. "What about Hilary?"

"I think she's in the waiting room."

Emily grabbed her purse. "She's probably scared to death! I'll follow you there."

A flicker of surprise and respect flashed through Beau's eyes before he nodded and shrugged. "Okay."

Emily pulled the slice-and-bake cookies from the oven and smiled at the sight of Hilary tottering in a pair of Emily's high heels. Dressed in a sapphire blue sequined cocktail dress Emily had planned to wear on her honeymoon, the little girl adjusted the tiara on her head. It had required a swift in-depth review of her early childhood, but Emily had been able to successfully distract the child.

"When did you get this crown?" Hilary asked.

Emily smiled. "It's called a tiara, but we can call it a crown. My mother is very beautiful. She is so beautiful that when she was younger she used to win beauty contests, and they gave her tiaras.''

Hilary studied Emily. ''You're pretty, too. Did you win a contest and get a crown?''

Emily laughed and shook her head. With a spatula, she removed the warm cookies from the sheet. ''My mother gave me that crown to play with when I was a little girl. I didn't win any contests. Although she tried her best,'' she muttered to herself, shuddering at the memory of being primped and coached for hours.

''Why didn't you win?''

Glancing at the child, Emily took the plate of cookies in one hand and Hilary's hand in the other and led her into the front living room. ''Why didn't I win?'' she repeated, sitting on the sofa. ''Three very good reasons.''

Outside the screen door, despite the sadness of the Bells' situation, Beau felt the slightest jab of amusement. He cocked his mouth into a half grin at the exchange between the two females. He might have expected Emily to be too fussy about her clothes to let a little girl trot around in them. But he would have underestimated her. Again.

Pausing, he decided to watch the two for just a couple more moments. Besides he was curious to learn why Emily hadn't won any contests.

''Two of the reasons,'' Emily told Hilary as she lifted her hair, ''are my ears. I got my father's ears.''

Hilary was silent for a moment as she munched her cookie. ''I like your ears. They remind me a little bit of Dumbo, the Baby Elephant.''

Emily let out a throaty laugh, and Beau felt the sexy purr deep in his gut.

"Why, thank you," she said. "No one has ever said that to me before. The third reason I didn't win was because I also inherited my father's musical talent."

"Musical?" Hilary echoed, confusion evident in her voice.

"He was very good at listening to music, but he wasn't good at making it."

Beau chuckled again and tapped on the door. "Emily, it's Beau."

She moved quickly, and he sensed an immediate change in her easy demeanor as she opened the door. Her eyebrows drew together in concern. "How is Regina?" she whispered.

The heaviness of the day hit him again. "She's going to be okay. Two cracked ribs and some bad bruises, but she signed a warrant for her husband's arrest," he told her in a low voice as he stepped into the room. "She remembered you offered to keep Hilary for the night, but she asked me to make sure it was okay. They're keeping her overnight at the hospital. She'll pick up her daughter tomorrow."

"Of course," Emily said, and looked at Hilary. "The sheriff says your mommy is going to be okay and will be leaving the hospital tomorrow. Would you mind staying with me tonight?"

Staring at Beau, Hilary bit her lip. "Okay."

Seeing the fear in the little girl's eyes, Beau knelt down next to the couch. "Any chance I can have one of those cookies?"

Tentatively she lifted one from the plate and offered it to him as if he were a wild animal not to be trusted.

"Thank you," he said in the gentlest voice he could muster, and silently damned Hilary's father to hell for distorting her view of men. The child wore no visible bruises, but it would take a long time to heal the inner scars.

"I think it's getting close to bedtime," Emily said and gathered the little girl in her arms. "I'll be back in a minute. Help yourself to the cookies," she told him.

"I don't have a nightie," Hilary told her.

"I'll let you use one of mine," Emily told her, as she carried her toward the steps.

"I don't have a bed."

"You can use mine."

"I don't got a toothbrush," Hilary's voice carried back to him.

"I have an extra one," Emily reassured her.

Almost thirty minutes later Emily returned to the living room and sank down on the sofa. "I wonder who taught that child the game of twenty questions."

Beau studied her, liking her disheveled appearance. With her hair mussed and blouse pulled loose from her skirt, she looked more touchable. Even at this moment his fingers itched to feel the satin smoothness of her skin. He would have liked to pull her into his lap and play with her hair. "You could have sung her to sleep."

Emily shot him a dark look. "I didn't want to give her nightmares."

"Your father's musical talent?"

"Tone deaf," she told him. "I sing in the shower, for my ears only."

"Speaking of your ears," he began.

Her blue eyes accused him. "You were listening."

"I didn't want to interrupt," he said, and leaned closer.

She looked at him suspiciously. "What are you doing?"

Giving in to the urge to lift her hair, Beau grinned. Emily's ears weren't large, but they did stick out. "I never would have compared them to Dumbo's."

She swatted at his hand. "Stop! I don't make a habit of showing my ears to the general public." She laughed despite herself. "I'd rather reveal my bra size."

Beau felt her throaty laugh again, this time in his groin. "I already know your bra size."

"I think you already know too much."

"There's where you're wrong, Emily. I want to know more," he told her. "A whole lot more."

Six

Emily stared into Beau's dark eyes and felt herself melt: her heart, her mind, her resolve. How did he do that so easily, she wondered. She took a careful breath and tried to make her brain work.

Though she suspected Beau wasn't all that interested in her statistics, she couldn't think of anything else to say to break the tension between them. "I'm twenty-five, an only child," she managed in a voice that sounded husky to her own ears. "You probably heard my mother was a beauty queen. My father died in an automobile accident when I was six."

Beau blinked and backed slightly away. "My father died when I was eight. Accident on a tractor."

She identified with the quick grief that flashed through Beau's eyes. Even after all these years, she still felt the loss of her father. "That must have been difficult for you. Only son with three sisters and mother."

"It was no picnic," he admitted. "How was it for you?"

Emily smiled sadly. "He made my mother and me laugh. She could have married any number of men, but he made her laugh. She always said my father was magic. He could find the humor in the blackest situation. When he died," she said, remembering those early, sad days, "my mother stopped laughing. I think it must have frightened her, so she became very protective and controlling."

Beau nodded thoughtfully. "And what about you? Do you miss him?"

"I was so young," she said, seeing mental pictures of her father. "I should be over it. Most of the time I don't brood over him. But there's this feeling of loss. It's not overwhelming," she told him quickly, "but it never goes away. It's like a hole and no one else will be able to fill it up."

Beau narrowed his eyes in disbelief at Emily. She'd said all the things he'd repeated to himself time and time again. He'd talked to others who had lost parents, but he'd never felt such a connection with them. It was almost as if she'd touched a sore spot inside him. And soothed it.

"Why are you staring at me?" she whispered.

He laughed to shake off the uneasy rumbling inside him. "Because you keep surprising me."

She lifted her hand toward his, then hesitated, meeting his gaze. Instinct, swift and sure, had him closing his hand around hers.

"Tell me about your father," she said.

A flood of memories rushed through him. "He was a farmer. His first love was the land, but he could ride like the wind."

"And he taught you?"

"Yeah, he taught me to ride, but he taught me other things, too. How to shoot. How to block a punch. He taught me to thank my mom when she fussed over my scratches and scrapes and put on Band-Aids. He helped me catch my first fish. He told me a real man says he's sorry when he's wrong, and if someone needs help to give it, because you might be the one needing help someday."

"He sounds like he must have been great."

"Yes. He just left too soon."

Emily closed her eyes. "I know what you mean. I feel lucky—" she shrugged "—blessed, that I knew my father as long as I did. But another part of me can't help wishing I could have had him just a little longer. There's so much I would have loved to talk with him about."

Beau looked at Emily again and felt a curious lump in his throat. She was doing it again. Saying what he'd thought, what he'd kept to himself. "A few times, when I got myself into some messes, it was easy for me to imagine what he would say."

She opened her eyes and smiled. "What?"

"Boy, you must have left your head in bed this morning!"

She laughed softly, then was quiet and thoughtful for a moment. "You'll think I'm crazy if I tell you this."

Beau looked at her curiously. "What?"

She shook her head and tried to pull her hand from his. "No. You'll think I'm nuts."

Beau held on to her hand. "What? Tell me." When she just looked at him sheepishly, he lowered his face closer to hers. "I already *know* you're a little crazy, Emily. What do you have to lose?"

She rolled her eyes. "Gee thanks, Beau." She took a deep breath. "Okay. Sometimes, when I'm all alone and I'm having a tough time, I talk to him."

Stunned, Beau just stared at her silently.

"I told you you'd think I was crazy! He doesn't really answer back," she quickly assured Beau. "I'm sure it won't make a bit of sense to you, but it makes me feel better, especially if I've been upset." She glanced at Beau again. "I wish you would quit looking at me like I belong in the loony bin."

Beau tugged her closer. "You misunderstand," he told her. "If you're crazy, then I am, too. I've talked to my father since he's been gone, too."

Her blue eyes met his. "Does he talk back?"

Beau shook his head. "No, but if he did, I know what he would tell me to do right now."

"What?"

"He'd say 'shut up and kiss the girl.' And, Emily, the older I get, the more I appreciate his advice." Beau took her mouth and was struck by the power and sweetness of her. Pulling her onto his lap, he felt so hungry for her that he wanted to eat her alive.

Instead, he made love to her mouth. A primitive instinct to claim urged him to thrust inside her, but Beau focused on the texture of her lips, the taste of her tongue. He coaxed the inhibitions from her and drew out her response.

She wiggled in his lap and he fought back a groan. Beau was hard and wanting. His arousal more than physical, he'd never experienced such an overwhelming need for a woman. It was all over him, his skin, his blood, his heart and lungs, his loins. He needed *Emily*. It was as if his body was calling out for her.

Driven to possess, he opened her mouth with his tongue and claimed her with carnal, sexual kisses while he slid one hand over her breast and the other beneath her skirt. She was caught up in the same sensual whirlwind he was. He knew it by the way she sucked his tongue into her mouth, rubbed her thighs against his hand, and undulated her bottom against his hardness.

He could feel it in the distended peak of her breast against his palm. He could hear it in her breath: soft gasps that urged him onward. He slipped his fingers beneath her silk panties and found her wet and hot.

"Oh, Emily, you feel so good," he muttered against her mouth. He stroked her silken secrets and eased his finger inside her at the same time he plunged his tongue into her mouth. In and out he stroked, simulating the intimacy he craved with her.

She shuddered and a soft whimper escaped her parted lips. She was clinging to him as if she couldn't let go. His chest swelled at the deep-down knowledge.

"Pull me closer, sweet lady," he whispered. "Let me inside." He'd never admitted he was lonely, even to himself, but he had been. And Emily could take his "lonely" away. "Let me inside," he repeated, still stroking her intimately.

Emily shuddered again. Her eyelids drooped, as heavy as the arousal pulsing between them. She dipped her head. "Beau. I—" She gasped and tightened her fingers on his shoulders.

He could tell when reality hit her. Her eyes widened and her soft thighs went rigid against his arm. She swallowed audibly and shook her head.

Though it cost him, he had to respond to her withdrawal. He moved his hand from her sweetness and lifted her chin so she would meet his gaze. "You want me," he said. He wanted to hear the words.

She clenched her eyes shut. "I—shouldn't. I—"

A primitive need to possess roared through him. "You want to be with me. Admit it," he demanded.

"I shouldn't," she wailed. "I was going to marry another man just weeks ago. I *can't* want to be with another man so soon. I *can't.*"

The shame in her voice was a balm to his frustrated need. She was nearly crying. He pulled her against him, cuddling her head against his chest. "You didn't really want him, Emily. Not like you want me."

"Oh, Beau," she said, clinging to him. "I can't want you right now. I just can't."

Minutes later Beau left, and Emily was left with a burning ache, a terrible emptiness. She instinctively put her hand to her chest where she felt tight, yet hollow. The hurt was so strong it was physical.

Taking a deep breath, she walked upstairs to check on Hilary as she slept. She watched the little girl for a few moments, then returned to her small kitchen and began to pace. If someone had told her last week that she could want a man this much, she would have told them they were crazy. It was insane to feel this much desire. Unreasonable. Illogical. Completely irrational.

Yet she did.

Emily shook her head. "There he goes," she muttered darkly. "Shifting my platelets again."

She sighed, feeling betrayed by her own body. The tips of her breasts were still hard. Deep down where he'd touched her, she was still wet and swollen. When Beau had left he'd looked too calm, too sure, for her peace of mind. He looked like a man who understood the inevitable and also understood that it was only a matter of time before Emily accepted the inevitable, too.

Be careful.

Let her rip.

Emily felt the tug and pull of her friends' words. They echoed the opposing instincts at war inside her. She wasn't the same woman she'd been when she'd blown into town three weeks ago. She wasn't as reserved. She was more impatient, more restless, less careful. The knowledge disturbed her.

At the same time she took the man's order for another pitcher of beer, Emily felt a buzzing sensation at the back of her neck. She glanced toward the door and saw Beau enter the room. Her heart jumped and her mind scowled. His gaze met hers, and she tentatively lifted her hand to wave at him.

He nodded and walked toward her. Then a woman stepped in his path and hooked her arm through his.

Beau glanced at Emily again, shrugging as he allowed himself to be led to the woman's table.

Holding an empty beer pitcher, Emily stood staring at them for a full minute. There was an easiness between them, she thought, a *physical* easiness. As if they were friends. Another image flashed through her mind. As if they were more than friends. The notion sliced through her like a sharp knife, surprising her with the quick stab of pain.

"Hey, sweet cakes! Where's my beer?"

The voice snapped her out of her daze. "Just a minute, please," she said, and she returned to the bar.

Since she'd started her temporary position for the county, Emily didn't work every night at the Happy Hour Bar. She had just started getting the hang of deflecting marriage proposals, so she hated the idea of completely giving it up. If she was going to run into Beau and his lady friend at the bar, however, she didn't know if she would have the stomach for it.

There was no rational reason for her to feel jealous, she told herself. She and Beau had certainly never made any promises to each other. They hadn't even gone out on a date. If she had felt closer to him last night than she'd ever felt to another human being, then that was her problem. He clearly didn't share the same perspective. She wouldn't give it another thought, she told herself.

Her gaze returning to Beau and *that woman,* Emily automatically filled a pitcher. She wondered if it was Donna.

Emily bit back a groan. Okay, she felt curious and jealous, she admitted. If there was one thing her mother had given her, however, it was the training to conceal everything from a pimple, to under-eye circles, to every disturbing emotion known to womankind.

Emily smiled.

From across the bar, Beau heard Donna continue her mostly one-sided conversation. He nodded every ten seconds or so, but he'd lost the thread of the conversation minutes ago. His attention was focused on the blond waitress bestowing a dazzling smile on every guy within ten feet of her.

Beau frowned.

"You want to come back to my place?" Donna murmured in an inviting voice next to his ear.

The suggestion should have been a turn-on. He waited to feel the slow, easy pump of arousal and excitement. Donna was attractive and intelligent. Any man in his right mind would take her up on what she was offering. *Any man in his right mind...* He waited for just a flicker of interest and was alarmed when he felt none. He would have to think about that later.

Beau cleared his throat and tapped his empty glass. "I think I need a refill. Let me get one for you, too," he offered, then took their glasses and made his way to the counter. By way of Emily.

"How did the training go today?" he asked, and noticed that her smile slipped a little. "I wasn't in the office much and I wondered how Mrs. Bing would handle the computer."

"Very well. I have all the basic instructions printed out for quick referral, and I found a template for the word-processing program. It went so well," she continued, setting a pitcher of beer down and giving another customer her dazzling smile, "that I'm going to let her train you and your deputy."

That announcement jolted Beau. He raised his eyebrows. "I thought you were supposed to train everyone."

"Well, I was, but Mrs. Bing caught on so well it seemed a waste for me to stay on."

Amazed at the disappointment that shot through him, he followed her to the counter. "So you're not coming back?"

She shrugged. "I guess that depends on the county. I think I'm a cyber fireman. They're putting me wherever they're having problems, then as soon as I solve those problems, they move me to the next one." She glanced at the glasses in his hands. "Would you like me to refill those for you?"

"Uh, yeah."

Emily returned the filled glasses to him with a smile. "There you go."

"Thanks," he said, studying her facial expression. Something wasn't quite right. "You look busy tonight."

Her eyes flashed something dark and secret. The emotion came and went so quickly it was as if someone had pulled apart the curtains in her bedroom, then jerked them back together. "*You* look pretty busy yourself tonight," she said, then whirled on to the next customer.

Beau hesitated, narrowing his gaze at her. If he didn't know better, he'd say Emily was a little green about Donna. But Emily had turned him down. Twice now. He shook his head and dismissed the possibility.

A woman ready, willing, and able to take care of his physical needs was waiting for him. And he was gaping after the one who kept saying no. He was not in his right mind. Beau headed toward the woman who was ready to say yes.

Frustrated, confused and unwilling to go home after work, Emily went to the lake again. She cut her engine, got out of her BMW and walked toward the water. It was a muggy night; the air was thick with heat and humidity, making most humans feel damp and uncomfortable. Emily was no exception.

She lifted her hair from her neck and continued to look at the lake as if it could offer her answers. She thought about all the things she'd always wanted to do but hadn't. Her mother had, at least temporarily, cut Emily out of her life. It was crazy, but the action both freed and hurt Emily. Now her choices were her own. She was responsible for what she did and didn't do. If there was a niggling thought that she couldn't run away forever, then Emily could temporarily brush it aside.

If she wanted to serve beer in a bar, she could. If she wanted to baby-sit a little girl named Hilary, she could. If she wanted to make love with a bad-boy sheriff... She hesitated and swore under her breath, glaring at the water again.

An idea came to mind. If she wanted to break the law by going to the lake at night, she could. If she wanted to wade at the edge of the lake on a hot summer night...

She could.

* * *

Beau wasn't sure if it was instinct or insanity that led him to the lake. Technically, he wasn't on duty, so he didn't need to cruise the area. When he saw Emily's BMW, however, the excitement he'd sought in vain earlier that evening hit him full-force.

He scowled at himself. He should either drive past or call the deputy to arrest her. Instead, he brought his truck to a stop and got out. Slamming the car door because it made him feel better, he took a deep breath and walked toward the lake.

The splashing sound stopped him mid-step. He quickly scanned the surface of the lake and saw Emily's head bobbing on the surface. He paused to listen more closely and heard her laughing. Shaking his head, he continued down the slight hill.

He stopped again when he came across the little pile of her clothes. Her lace bra and panties lay on top. His internal temperature rose, and Beau tugged at his shirt collar. What was he going to do with this woman? He heard her blowing bubbles. She obviously didn't realize she had an audience.

"How's the water, Emily?"

The blowing noises ceased, and Beau heard a strangled, choking sound. "You okay?"

When she didn't say anything, he became concerned. "Emily, answer me. Do I need to come after you and—"

"No!" she yelled, and swam closer so he could see her.

"Are you having a good time?" he asked mildly.

Brief silence met his question. She frowned at him. "I was."

He swallowed a chuckle at her prissy use of the past

tense. Her hair was slicked back from her face, and her shoulders gleamed in the moonlight. She looked like a water goddess—a peeved water goddess. "Do you remember that you're not supposed to trespass after dark at the lake?"

"I'm not really trespassing," she told him in the finishing-school voice she reserved for sticky situations.

"Oh really," he said. "Then tell me what you are doing?"

"I'm performing an important service to the community," she told him. "I'm making sure it's safe to swim in the lake."

"And have you?"

"Oh yes," she said, her first smile breaking through, the same dazzling smile she'd thrown at umpteen men back at the bar. "It's as safe as can be."

"Then your job is done," Beau said, catching her with her own net. "You can come out now."

Her smile fell. "I—I haven't had a chance to check—"

"Emily, if my deputy decides to patrol the lake tonight, which he always does, he will arrest you for trespassing and take you in buck-naked." He leaned over and picked up her panties. "I don't know how much tequila you got into tonight, but—"

"I haven't had a drop of tequila since the first night I was in town!" she told him.

"Then why are you acting like you have?"

"This was just one of those little harmless things I've never done but wanted to do. It would have been fine if you hadn't stopped by."

"Harmless," he echoed. "Harmless like tossing your ring into the lake—"

"I didn't do that," she retorted.

"And sleeping on black satin sheets," he continued, watching her shift in the water. "Driving a motorcycle, riding a horse, lighting a man's cigar in bed and—"

"The least you can do is turn around while I get out," she said, frustration oozing from her voice.

Beau thought of how many nights the image of Emily, naked and wanting him, had made him sweat with unfulfilled need. He remembered how she took him to the edge with her kisses, then pulled back. He thought of how she'd seduced his attention so that he couldn't muster the least bit of interest in other women. Any compassion or sense of decency he might have had dissolved.

"No," he simply said.

She gasped. "Beau—"

He shook his head and picked up her bra. "It seems to me, Emily, that you haven't had enough excitement in your life, so you're determined to make up for it now. I consider it my duty to help you."

"Help me," she repeated, her voice full of skepticism.

"Yes. With your upbringing, I'll bet you missed out on a little game we played when we were growing up."

She frowned. "Little game."

"Yeah. It's called Take the Dare. I dare you to walk out of the lake." He lifted her bra to his face and inhaled the faint scent of her perfume. "Come to me, Emily."

Seven

Emily sank beneath the water's surface. The one time she decides to go skinny-dipping, the sheriff catches her. Maybe she should just drown herself, she thought darkly. Instead, she emerged and sucked in a breath of air. His voice was entirely too inviting. She couldn't make out much more than the outline of his body, but she could easily imagine the dare in his dark eyes. She could easily imagine her entire bare body turning pink beneath his gaze.

"Come to me," Beau repeated in a seductive tone that made her glad she wasn't standing, because her knees wouldn't have supported her. Dracula had probably used the same words when he lured his victims.

Shivering both from the cool temperature of the water and her apprehension, she realized she wouldn't be able to outlast Beau. She closed her eyes briefly and made a quick promise to herself that it would all be over in a couple of minutes. She would walk out of the water, pull on her clothes as quickly as possible and go to her car.

Taking a deep breath, Emily walked toward Beau with as much dignity as she could muster. She refused to look at his face, keeping her eyes focused on the ground for her clothes. A terrible panic invaded her when she didn't spot them and she was forced to meet Beau's gaze.

He swore.

She saw her clothes in his hands. "I need my clothes."

He swore again.

Her panic spiked. "I need my clothes, Beau!"

As if to shake himself from a daze, he gave a quick jerk of his head. "Yeah, you do. Come here."

"I don't think so," she told him, through chattering teeth.

"Come here," he said in a tone that allowed no disagreement. "I'll help you get dressed."

She simply stared at him as he stepped closer to her, slung some of her clothes over his shoulder, and pulled out her bra.

"Come on. Put your arms through. You're freezing."

Emily did as he said, still astounded that he was *dressing* her. The backs of his fingers burned as he brushed them under her breasts to fasten the front of her bra. He could have fondled her breasts and caressed her nipples. The almost-touch of his hands sent her temperature soaring.

He bent slightly and held out her panties for her to step into. He could have stroked her thighs and slipped his fingers between her legs where she was moist. Her thighs trembled, her heart tripped at the strange intimacy of his actions. There was something tenderly erotic about his attitude. She could feel his gaze on her. She could sense his need. It made her defenses as substantial as a house of cards.

"Why are you doing this?" she asked in a voice that sounded thin and wispy to her own ears as he buttoned her blouse.

"You were cold. You were naked," he muttered. "You needed to be dressed."

"But—"

Beau shook his head and held out her jeans. "Don't ask too many questions, Emily. You might not like the answers."

She braced herself on his shoulders, but after she pulled up her jeans, her fingers wouldn't cooperate when she tried to fasten them. He finished the job for her, and she was stunned at what she saw. "Look at your hands," she whispered. "They're shaking. Why?"

He inhaled quickly and backed away. "You really have no idea how beautiful you are, do you? You have no idea what the sight of your naked body can do to a man. No idea," he said, giving a forced, rough chuckle. "Get in your car, Emily. I'll follow you home."

His self-denial confused her. "But—"

He swore. "*Now*, Emily—"

Grabbing her shoes from the ground, she shrugged

and walked to her car, her mind awhirl at what Beau had just done for her, to her. Automatically she drove to her house, her mind stuck back at the lake with a sense of wonder. Why would a man do that? Touch her and yet not touch her?

When she pulled into her driveway and got out of her car, she struggled with a sense of inevitability. She saw him park at her curb and stand beside his truck. Her hair still damp, she walked toward Beau. A faint inner voice reminded her that she'd only met him a few weeks before. She didn't know him well. A stronger voice told her she knew what she needed to know about him.

His tension twisted around him like an overstretched rubber band. His eyes were narrowed as if he were angry at her, but she suspected his anger was directed at himself. Her stomach twisted with a mixed sense of destiny and apprehension. It was as if fate had brought her to this very place on this very night. With this very man.

"Go on in," he told her. "I'll leave after you lock up."

He was so accustomed to having his orders followed, she thought. She would have smiled if she hadn't felt so nervous. "No," she said.

He blinked. "Go on in, Emily," he said, his tone less gentle.

"No," she repeated. "I'm still cold."

He stared at her for a long moment and didn't move.

So she did. Stumbling forward, she flattened herself against his body and stretched her arms around him.

His posture rigid, Beau swore. "What are you doing?"

"Trying to get warm." *Trying to get close.*

He shuddered. "Emily, I've seen you. I can't go partway with you anymore."

Her heart was pounding so hard she wondered if it might burst. "Then don't," she said. "Take me all the way."

He went completely still. "What are you saying?"

She looked into his wary face. "I need to be close to you," she whispered. "As close as we can get."

An oath spilled from his mouth a breath before he closed his arms around her and kissed her. It was a claiming kiss that went on and on until Emily's head began to spin. Her knees dipped, and she stiffened them. She felt his hunger mirrored deep inside her.

"Let's go in," he muttered, then urged her toward the front door. She tried to put the key in the lock, but couldn't do more than jangle the key ring. He took over the job and had them inside within seconds, her back against the foyer wall, his mouth, hungry and demanding, on hers again. He discarded the clothes he'd so carefully put on her at the lake, and within moments she was naked.

Emily was hot inside, but her nerves made her feel cold on the outside. She wanted closer, and his shirt was in the way. Tugging at his buttons, she pushed it aside and slid her hands over his bare skin.

Closing his palm over her breast, he groaned. "Let's go upstairs, sweetheart," he murmured, then nipped at her earlobe.

Emily swallowed at the heady sense of anticipation

invading her body. Why did this feel so right? she wondered. "The sheets aren't satin."

He gave a muffled chuckle. "I won't be noticing the sheets." Then he swung her up into his arms and climbed the stairs to her bedroom. He took her mouth again and allowed her body to slowly slide down his until her toes touched the floor. She felt his hardness pressing insistently against the front of his jeans.

He opened his mouth and teased her with an almost-kiss, his lips against hers, then pulled away just when she started to respond. "Reach into my left pocket," he told her.

She slid her hand down and pulled out the plastic packet. She felt a rush of both chagrin and relief. Thank goodness *he'd* prepared. He plucked the packet from her fingers and tossed it on the bed. For a split second she thought about telling him this was her first time, but he kissed her again and put her hand on his belt, and her mind went blank.

Fumbling with his belt, she loosened it, then edged his zipper down, the hissing sound echoing inside her like a flame. She'd have thought she would feel awkward, but he made her feel as if it was the most natural thing in the world for her to be undressing a man.

He kicked off his shoes and pushed down his denims and briefs. Her heart jumped into her throat at the sight of him naked and fully aroused. His shoulders looked impossibly broad, his chest well muscled and defined, with a sprinkling of hair. His masculinity jutted proudly between his thighs. Meeting her gaze, he walked her backward toward the bed until the backs of her legs bumped the edge of the mattress. The sensual look in his eyes took her breath.

He brushed her hair back and gave a half grin. Catching her breath, she wondered how he managed to look both amused and aroused at the same time.

"I like your ears."

Groaning, Emily ducked her head into his chest, his soft hair tickling her warm cheeks. "Oh, did you *have* to mention them?"

"Yeah. They remind me that you're human. Everything else," he murmured, sliding his hands down the outer edge of her breasts to her waist and hips, "is perfect."

She shook her head. "Not perfect. Not perfect at all."

"Yeah it is. Dressed, you're pretty as a picture. Undressed," he said with a sigh, "you're perfect. Quit arguing with me," he said when she opened her mouth to do just that. "Kiss me instead."

The dare in his voice tickled something inside her, and she pressed her open mouth against his throat and licked him.

He swore. "Your mouth is incredible. I've had dreams when all I did was kiss you."

"Really?" She was surprised, secretly delighted.

"Really," he told her in a deep voice, and lifted his hands to her breasts. "And I've spent an inordinate amount of time thinking about your nipples." He plucked her beaded tips until she felt a pull deep down between her thighs. Lowering his head, he sucked her into his mouth, laving her with his tongue.

Emily clung to his shoulders and bit back a moan.

She felt like a whirlpool of sensation, spinning, sinking.

He slid one of his hands down between her legs and found her where she was moist and sensitive. "Oh, Beau."

"You're wet," he said, and fondled her with breathtaking persistence. "There's so much I want to do with you, but I don't think I'm gonna be able to wait long tonight. I feel like I've been waiting half a lifetime already."

His need for her accelerated her own. He slipped one finger inside her, making her gasp. "Touch me," he told her in a husky voice.

Eager to arouse him as he'd aroused her, she wrapped her hand around him. He slid gently within her hand and stroked her intimately at the same time. It was erotic to see him so turned on, to know she was doing it to him. Her arousal spiked. Edgy, excited, she rubbed her thumb back and forth over the honeyed tip of his masculinity.

Beau closed his eyes and began to swear. "Emily, I want to be inside you."

"Yes," she whispered. She wanted that, too. She wanted him, all of him.

Gently nudging her backward, he followed her down on the bed. His body covered hers, his mouth took her lips, his arms were braced on either side of her, and she felt deliciously surrounded by him.

Pushing her legs apart, he caressed her until she couldn't stay still beneath his fingers. His tongue teased and taunted, sucking hers into his mouth as if he couldn't get enough of her. He touched her as if everything about her delighted him.

She was hot, reaching for him, reaching for something inside her. She stared into his dark, sexy eyes. "Beau—"

"What, sweetheart?" he muttered, nuzzling her neck.

"I need—" She wriggled beneath him, still reaching.

"You need what?"

"Oh." She arched against him. "You."

Beau groaned, and she felt him shift. Pushing her thighs farther apart, he held her with his gaze and thrust inside her.

Emily felt a burning sensation inside her. She watched Beau's eyes widen at the same time hers did. He started to pull back, and she instinctively tightened her thighs around him.

His nostrils flared. "You—you—"

She took a careful breath and licked her suddenly dry lips. "I meant to tell you, but I forgot."

Still poised just inside her, he studied her. "Forgot?" he asked in a voice he clearly struggled to keep neutral.

"I haven't done this before," she admitted.

His nostrils flared again. "You're a virgin."

Her body accommodated him and she wiggled experimentally. "Was. You feel big."

He swore, then chuckled roughly. "You feel incredible. Incredible." He lifted his hand to her cheek and looked at her with a sense of wonder. "Why didn't you tell me?"

He was inside her, but she wanted more. She was still reaching. "You, uh, distracted me."

He shook his head. "Oh, Emily," he murmured, then slid the rest of the way inside her.

She undulated beneath him, revelling in the full sensation. "You still feel very big."

His mouth tilted into a sexy grin. "Is that bad?"

Restless, she shook her head and arched into him. "Beau?"

"Yeah." He kissed her, distracting her again for a moment.

"Take me all the way," she whispered.

In an instant his eyes changed, his body tensed. "Hold on." Then he took her with fluid, sensual thrusts, pumping inside her. With each long stroke, he rubbed a sensitive spot deep inside her, making her tighten and cling to him.

"You're so good, Emily. Let it go," he urged her.

Again and again, he pumped until she jerked, the tension inside her bursting like stars. She thought it was all over, but he kept on and she burst again, whimpering his name.

Writhing, she flexed around him, staring into his eyes as he went over the top. Holding her tight, he cradled her as if, for that single glorious moment, she was his world. And Emily knew she would never be the same.

Beau pulled the covers loose and dragged them over their cooling bodies. He took a careful breath and looked at the woman who, for the last three weeks, had disturbed his waking and sleeping hours. She looked dazed and thoroughly loved, her mouth swollen from his kisses. He was stunned to see faint marks on her fair skin.

Pushing his hair back from his damp forehead, he struggled to get perspective. His emotions were all over the place. At the same time he felt protective of Emily, he was scared spitless of her. The woman had turned him upside down. Rather than defusing his hunger for her, making love had only made him want her more.

She lifted her fingers to his mouth and looked at him with a searching gaze. "How many hundreds of women line up outside your door to ask you to make love to them?"

Her question was so ridiculous and flattering that it temporarily pushed back his uneasiness. "None," Beau said, shaking his head. "This was your first time, Emily. Why me?"

Her eyelashes fluttered down, shielding her expression from him. She shifted as if she wasn't totally sure of herself. "I'm not sure how to explain it, but I've never felt as close to anyone as I have you. I felt a connection. It doesn't really make sense, but it felt right." She gave a hard sigh. "It seemed right to be with you."

She glanced up at him quickly, then away again. "I thought you felt the same way. Maybe I was wrong. Maybe it was just me and—"

He pressed his mouth over hers to silence her doubts. Despite his own confusion, Beau couldn't let her think he didn't feel the same *connection*. "I did. It was different for me, too."

Of its own volition, his body began to respond to her again. His skin still burned, he was hard, primed to take her yet again. And he'd just taken her.

He could spend the night touching her, sipping kisses from her lips, sliding between her thighs, making her sigh and moan. He could, he thought, spend more than a night. The thought disturbed him. The feelings deep inside him disturbed him even more.

The sight of her bare body aroused him, but it was the way she responded to him, the way she so obviously wanted him. It was her personality, her trust, that urged him to get inside her. To stay.

Frowning thoughtfully, Beau decided he should go. He needed to get a grip. Besides, there were other considerations. He pulled her closer and kissed the top of her head, surprised at the force of his desire to stay. He'd never wanted to stay all night with a woman before.

"I can't stay," he told her while she snuggled against him. "The bad thing about being sheriff is everyone knows my truck. If my truck is here in the morning, everyone will know I've stayed all night."

Emily stilled and was silent for a long moment. She pulled away, and Beau felt the gap more than physically.

Brushing her hair from her face, she didn't meet his gaze. "I hadn't thought of that. It must be difficult for you."

He resisted the urge to pull her back into his arms. Barely. "It can be."

She paused, clutching the sheet as if she wanted to

wrap it around her. Then she moved to rise from the bed.

Beau felt an inexplicable sting of regret. He stopped her, wrapping his fingers around her wrist. ''Emily—'' he began.

''I just need to get my robe so I can walk you to the door,'' she said, tugging ineffectually. Her blue gaze finally met his. ''You said you need to go.''

In her eyes, he saw no censure, no accusation. But she couldn't hide the vulnerability. Biting back an oath, he released her and rose from the bed, too.

She practically flew to the closet and wrapped her robe around her as he pulled on his jeans and shirt. He shoved his feet into his shoes, all the while hating the silent tension building between them.

They walked down the stairs, and it would have been the most natural thing in the world for him to take her hand, but something stopped him. When they reached the foyer, he looked at her. ''I'll call you to—''

''You don't have to,'' she blurted out, rendering him speechless.

Eight

Beau stared at her.

Unable to dodge him, Emily met his don't-try-to-fool-me gaze. Her heart twisted, but she tried for a casual shrug. She'd just been through the most powerful, moving experience of her life, and she felt as if she was holding herself together by a thread.

"No. Really," she insisted, trying to sound rational when she felt anything but. "I understand that just because we made love doesn't necessarily change our relationship. You're very committed to not being committed to a woman, and I don't expect you to act differently with me." Feeling her cheeks heat, she couldn't bring herself to use the word *arrangement*, but she forged on. "I don't want you to think that since I'm not experienced I expect something you don't want to give."

He let her statement hang between them for a long moment. "You don't think anything's changed between us after making love?" he asked in that silk and stone voice.

"I didn't say that. I said I didn't expect you—"

He shook his head. "I heard you. Now you hear me. I'll call you tomorrow." He bent down to kiss her firmly on the lips, then backed away. "Everything between us is changed. *Everything.*"

From the expression on his face, Emily wasn't sure that was good or bad.

By morning Emily was searching for her inner calm. The problem, she'd determined, was that she didn't have any instructions on how to deal with Beau. No etiquette books offered practical tips for this situation. Advice to the lovelorn might provide something, but Emily wasn't exactly *lorn.* Loony perhaps, but not lorn.

She didn't regret making love with him. How could she regret such a beautiful, powerful experience? How could she regret the moments that had brought her a feeling of such connection to another human being? She couldn't, but she wasn't exactly sure where things between Beau and her would go now.

Heaven knows, he didn't want commitment, and she wasn't ready. After all, she'd been walking down the aisle to marry another man just one month ago. Emily cringed at the thought. She needed the perspective time would bring. Every day made her see things a little differently. The last few days she'd felt a fleeting inclination to pay a quick visit to Roanoke. Perhaps that would give her a sense of resolution, she thought, but dismissed the possibility when it filled her heart with dread.

None of her thoughts diminished the disconcerting vulnerability she felt this morning. She felt stripped naked. The fact that she was scheduled to join Beau's sisters and their families for Sunday dinner today at Rosemary's was almost enough to give her a case of the hives.

She considered begging off, but pride wouldn't allow it. Taking some solace in the fact that Beau rarely joined his sisters for Sunday dinner, she pulled herself together and went. Helping Rosemary with last-minute preparations for dinner distracted her until Beau walked in just as everyone sat down at the table.

She looked at him, and her feeling of vulnerability shot to the surface. He sat directly across from her. Giving him a forced, light greeting, she bowed her head for the blessing and felt his gaze on her. Too conscious of his attention, she pushed her food around her plate and made conversation with Caroline's husband. It irritated her how difficult she found it to carry on a simple conversation just because Beau was in the same room.

He was just a man, she told herself.

Just a man who had touched her heart and taken her body. A man who had made her loneliness go away.

Emily swore under her breath. She didn't want Beau to matter that much to her. She didn't want to care about him. She concentrated harder.

"Want some salt?" Beau offered the shaker.

"Thank you." Emily automatically accepted it,

holding her breath when he stroked her fingers before he released the shaker.

"You haven't eaten much," he said.

She swallowed. "I'm not very fast."

His gaze darkened and swept down to her mouth. "That's okay. Slow is better."

Her heart raced and she prayed her cheeks weren't as red as the homegrown tomatoes in her salad. When he said *slow*, he wasn't talking about eating dinner. A shudder of awareness ran through her.

She deliberately turned her attention to Rosemary and Valene's discussion about their favorite cousin's upcoming wedding.

"Her fiancé's going to be shipped out on a nuclear submarine, and they want to tie the knot before he leaves."

"They only have a week," Valene added. "I feel so sorry for Annie. She won't have time to get a special dress or anything."

"She's such a little thing, like Emily. It's hard for her to buy off the rack," Caroline explained.

A thought struck Emily. "Do you think she could wear my wedding dress?"

Rosemary gasped. "Don't you want to save it?"

Emily shrugged. "For what?"

Rosemary looked uncomfortable. "Well, if you decide to get married again."

Everything within Emily rebelled at the idea. "No," she said and hoped that would be enough.

When she saw the expectant expressions of Beau's three sisters, though, she could tell it wouldn't be enough. "I think weddings are wonderful," she told them, *"for other people."*

"The first time we met, you mentioned something about not wanting to get married again, but that was an emotional moment, and you'd had a rough night before—"

"It wasn't," Emily said to Rosemary as gently as possible, "the tequila talking. I think it's marvelous for other people to get married. But I don't know when I'll be interested in getting married." Not daring to look at him even once, she wondered if she was saying that as much for Beau as for herself. She wondered if she was trying to prove something to him.

Bridging the silence, Valene cleared her throat. "It's very generous of you to offer your beautiful dress for Annie when you haven't even met her. That says a lot about what a kind person you are."

Emily felt her cheeks heat. "It's nothing. Really, I—"

"Stop trying to deny it," Caroline said. "We'll call Annie after lunch and she can see about alterations. I'm sure she'll be delighted."

"I'm headed out that direction later today if you'd like me to take it," Beau offered.

Tom snickered. "That's about as close as you'll get to a wedding dress. Sounds like you and Emily have the same attitude."

"Sounds like it," Beau said in a mild voice.

Feeling like a fraud, Emily met Beau's amused gaze. She supposed now wasn't the best time to tell everyone she'd considered burning her wedding gown so she wouldn't have to look at it anymore. Now also wasn't the time to mention that she and Beau shared more than an attitude. They'd shared her bed, their bodies, and at least part of their hearts.

She felt his feet stretch to either side of hers, lightly trapping her, as if he were determined to remind her of their intimacy. Did he really think she needed to be reminded?

She forced down a few more bites, and dinner was almost over when Valene addressed her again. "Emily, I recall your mentioning that you were involved in charity work in Roanoke, and I was wondering if you would join the Friends of the Library. We're meeting Tuesday night to brainstorm a fund-raiser."

Emily regretfully shook her head. "I'm sorry I can't on Tuesday night. I'm keeping Regina Bell's daughter, Hilary, two nights this week."

Rosemary made a tsking sound. "How is Regina? That situation is such a shame."

"Regina's still bruised, but she's much better. I think she's trying to decide whether to stay in Ruxton or go back to Kentucky where her family lives. Her husband—" she continued, then broke off as she glanced at Beau.

"Is in custody," Beau said flatly and didn't elaborate.

Valene sighed. "I don't want you to back out of sitting for Hilary, but we could use your help. We thought about holding an auction, but we can't get donations from any of the businesses."

"Then hold a service auction," she suggested, recalling a successful event she'd coordinated last year.

"Service auction?"

"People donate services and you auction them off. You can combine it with a picnic to increase the turnout."

Valene looked confused. "What kind of services?"

"Anything. I'll start by donating two hours of computer consultation time. Someone with a truck can donate a couple of hours for light hauling. Teenagers can donate mowing lawns or baby-sitting. People can donate dinners. The way you get started is by asking someone visible and well-respected to donate something. Then you tell everyone else what they donated so it gently pressures them to participate, too."

"I wonder what visible person we should ask," Valene said.

"That's easy," Caroline said. "He's sitting at our table."

"Beau," Valene said with a smile.

Emily could practically feel his groan.

He set down his fork. "Offhand, I can't think of any services I can provide," Beau said.

"I'm sure most of the single female population would disagree," Caroline said dryly.

"Be serious, Caroline. What do you think Beau could do, Emily?"

Emily wished she could hold her glass of iced tea to her face. She sipped it instead.

Beau sat back in his chair and looked at her with an intimate glint in his eyes as if he knew everything that was going on inside her, as if he could see the blatant sexual images that raced through her head.

"Yeah, Emily," Beau said, his voice full of double

meaning. "Since you're the experienced one, what do you think I could do for the auction?"

Choking on her tea, she gave Caroline's husband a weak smile when he gently thumped her on the back. "Horseback riding lessons," she managed to say.

"Perfect!" Valene cooed, clapping her hands. "Beau hasn't given a riding lesson since his rodeo days." She beamed at Emily. "You're brilliant. Isn't she brilliant?"

Emily was stuck on Valene's other statement. *Beau hasn't given a riding lesson since his rodeo days.* He'd made an exception for her. Why? she wondered, searching his inscrutable gaze for answers and finding none.

Brilliant? Try clueless.

Forty-five minutes later, Beau was ringing Emily's doorbell. She opened the door. Just looking at her made him feel like he'd been punched.

"You said you would call."

He shrugged. "Call, visit. Same thing." He walked through the doorway and without pausing, pulled her to him.

"No, it's not," she corrected. "A call involves the telephone and distance."

"I wanted something more personal." Then because he'd waited entirely too long, he kissed her long and well. When he drew away, he was wanting her again. "Why wouldn't you look at me at dinner?"

"I didn't think you wanted anyone to know—" she took a deep breath "—about last night. About us.

Your sisters are perceptive. I was afraid I'd give it away."

His gut twisted at the vulnerable expression on her face, and he lifted his hand to her cheek. "I don't want to share you. I want this to be just between you and me."

She gave a tentative smile. "That won't be easy."

"Yeah, I know," he muttered and shut the door. He linked his fingers through hers and tugged her toward the sofa to sit. Lord, he hoped the intensity of his desire for her lessened. "I could barely keep my hands off you today at Rosemary's."

"I'm at a loss," she told him, her eyes wide with dismay. "I feel like I've gotten on a wild ride at the amusement park and I don't know where it's headed or when it will stop." She pulled away from him and rose from the sofa as if she couldn't keep still.

When he started to get up, she put up her hands. "No. Please stay where you are. I have a hard time thinking clearly when you get close and I want to get this said." She swept her hand through her hair. "I don't know if I can explain this, but I feel close to you, closer than I've felt to anyone else. And I felt that way before last night. I—" She stalled, looking at the ceiling for help. "That's why I wanted— No, *needed* to be with you." Her eyes crinkled in confusion. "But it doesn't make any sense. We haven't even been on a date."

He rose then. "We can change that."

Her gaze searched his. "Are you sure you want to?"

"Emily, come here."

She hesitated, regarding him warily, but she moved closer.

Taking her hand again, he was uncomfortable with the strength of his feelings. "I'm not making any promises and you aren't, either, but I'd be lying if I said I could get enough of you. I can't." Something inside him resisted expounding further, but her honesty demanded his. "It's more than sex, although I want you right now. I wanted you at Rosemary's. I wanted you as soon as we'd made love last night."

She blinked in amazement, her eyes flickering with fear. "I don't know about this, Beau. I don't know if I'm ready for you. It was just a month ago that I was ready to marry another man."

He'd spent the entire night thinking about the exact same thing. He gave a dry, humorless chuckle. "Do you have a choice?"

Her expression changed. She glanced away, then back at him. "I guess not." She dipped her head and took a deep breath. "So what's next?"

"How about dinner at my house?"

Her lips twitched and she slowly nodded. "Okay, Sheriff. I look forward to seeing how well you cook."

He laughed again, this time with humor, and pulled her back into the circle of his arms. "Yeah, you definitely make me cook." He kissed her lips and felt a tightness in his chest when she slipped her fingers through his hair.

"Monday okay?" he asked her. Why did she feel like sunshine in his arms?

She licked her lips, her eyes slightly dazed. "For what?"

"Dinner."

"Yes."

He slid his hands down to her bottom and nestled himself between her thighs. Why did everything about her mesh with him? He should learn the answers to these questions. He should settle his curiosity, so she wouldn't have such power over him. He would, he decided, and he would enjoy every minute with her. "What are you doing Wednesday?"

"Nothing."

"Friday?" he asked, nuzzling her neck.

"Nothing. Why?"

"Consider yourself booked," he told her, wanting closer. It was strange, but he felt the need to seal their agreement, to know her intimately again. This time, he would do better. He would pay attention and not lose control. "Are you going to let me make love to you now?"

She hesitated, and he felt the echo of her brief silence deep inside him. He read her easily. "What is it?"

She looked away, embarrassed.

"Emily, what is it?"

"Do you have to be in such a rush to leave afterward this time?" she asked, meeting his gaze. "It was hard being close and having you leave so quickly."

Beau's chest tightened again. It was just as she'd told him. She needed him as close as he could get. Other women had wanted his body, perhaps a material commitment from him, but none had been interested in his heart. If Beau didn't know better, he would say something inside him had just yelled "Timber!"

When he'd gone home last night, he'd felt full, yet empty, filled with an urgency to get back to Emily. "I'm in no rush to leave you," he told her. "No rush at all." In the back of his mind, though, there was something about her that conjured up uncertainty. He couldn't put his finger on it, but mixed in with his desire and need, there was a voice that told him not to count on her forever.

Beau brought in the steaks and watched Emily meandering around his den, studying his pictures. Her hands folded behind her, she leaned forward to study the charcoal sketch of him during his rodeo days. He waited for her to adjust the frame. But she didn't. She just kept looking.

Interesting, he thought. "Steaks are ready," he said.

She glanced up and smiled. "They look great. Everything looks great," she said gesturing toward the table. "What can I do to help?"

"Already done," he told her, pulling the potatoes and rolls from the oven and tossing them on the table. "C'mon over and let me feed you."

"I'm surprised you prepared the meal." She sat down and smiled.

"You were expecting?"

"Takeout," she confessed.

He scowled. "That's for sissies."

She laughed. "And broiling is for real men."

"You're a perceptive woman."

"You're just hoping I'll do the dishes."

He chuckled, surprised at how much he enjoyed her presence in his home. Beau truly enjoyed his privacy.

She was the exception that proved the rule, he decided. "You're a perceptive woman."

He poured the wine. "Have any of my sisters called you today?"

Emily shook her head. "No. Why?"

"I got calls from each of them asking why I'd stayed so late at your house last night. They wanted to know if I was *seeing* you."

"Oops. What did you say?" She lifted a bite of steak to her lips.

He could have gotten distracted just watching her eat. He shook his head. But he wouldn't. "I told them I didn't have any problems with my vision, I could see just about everyone." He rolled his eyes. "It worked with Rosemary and Valene."

"But not with Caroline."

"Yeah. I told her you'd just baked some cookies and I raided your cookie jar." He smiled. "It was true, in a manner of speaking."

She blushed, lifting her napkin to cover her face for a second, then dropped it. "You wonder why they drive you crazy, but you bring it on yourself."

With a deadpan gaze, he said, "My mother always told me I was a perfect brother."

"But what do your sisters say?"

He paused. "They think I could use some work. Speaking of which, what do you think of my house?" He dug into his own meal.

She sipped her wine. "It's nice. The pictures and furniture, they say a lot about your personality and interests."

This was a test. He shouldn't do it, he told himself.

It was a sure way to kill the attraction, but curiosity won. "What would you change about my house?"

A blank look crossed her face. She looked around. "Are you unhappy with it?"

"Not really."

She looked puzzled. "Do you want something different? To change the colors or something?"

He tilted his head, looking at her thoughtfully. "No."

She shrugged. "It's your house. If you're happy with it, then it's not necessary to change anything."

Oops. Beau felt a sinking sensation in his gut.

Nine

Emily passed the test.

Beau took a gulp of his wine. He'd expected the more typical feminine inclination to perform make-overs. Women seemed obsessed with fixing things, changing things just for the sake of changing them. Much to his chagrin, he'd learned that the women in his life often wanted to fix him.

He eyed her speculatively. "There must be something you would change, some suggestion you would make."

She met his gaze, looking slightly confused. "No," she said drawing out the word. "When I was growing up, my mother always wanted my room one way, and I wanted it another. I think it's important for people to have their own space and make it the way they like it. It's probably one of the reasons I'm enjoying my house right now.''

He nodded slowly, watching her eat again. He should have known she would have a different perspective. ''So you're discovering what you like for the first time.''

''It's fun, but it might be easier if I had an interesting previous occupation like the rodeo.''

''You don't need a previous occupation. All you need to do is figure out what you like.'' Her point of view raised more questions in his mind. ''If you think everyone should have their own space, then how do you blend things when people live together?''

She gave a wry smile. ''I guess that's one more advantage to not getting married. I don't have to blend.''

A nonanswer, Beau thought, and mulled it over during the rest of the meal. If she'd been another woman, digging beneath the surface wouldn't have been necessary. She appealed to him, he wanted her, she wanted him. That should have been enough, but for some reason, it wasn't.

After dinner they cleaned the dishes together and took a walk to the barn. ''The first night I was here,'' she told him, ''I didn't even know you had a barn and horses. I barely noticed when I left the next morning.''

''You weren't in the best condition then.''

She laughed lightly. ''No, but I can see why you would love this. You have your space, your privacy and a couple of horses.''

He leaned against a stall and watched her roam around the barn. She was dressed in a butter yellow shirtwaist dress that showed her curves; and the way she moved restlessly about reminded him of a butterfly. She held a sugar cube in her hand to give to Blue, but she was tentative.

"That sugar's gonna melt in your hand if you don't go ahead and give it to Blue," he told her.

"Okay," she said and walked closer. "And you're sure he won't bite."

"I'm sure." Standing close to her, he put his hand under hers. "Hold your palm out flat. Watch him. He'll take it with his lips."

She did as he instructed and slowly lifted her hand toward the horse. She let out a muffled squeak when Blue took the cube.

Beau chuckled. "Did he steal a kiss?"

Shaking her hand, she smiled sheepishly at him. "I don't know. If he did, he must take after his owner."

Beau pulled her into his arms and drew in the soft clean scent of her light hair. "Butterfly. Flutterby."

She looked up at him curiously. "Butterfly, flutterby?"

He brushed his hand through her hair. "In that yellow dress with your light hair and the way you were flitting around, you reminded me of a butterfly. My father used to switch the syllables around."

The years rolled back to a special moment Beau remembered. "I liked catching butterflies when I was a kid. It was a major disappointment when I'd trap them in a glass jar and they would die. My father told me flutterbys were fun to chase, fun to catch and hold for a while. But you had to let 'em go."

His gaze met hers, and it finally struck him. The

niggling doubt in the back of his mind about Emily had its roots in a memory of his father.

Emily seemed to sense his tension. "What would your father have thought of me?"

"He would have thought you were pretty and sweet. Special," Beau said.

"But he also might have thought I was a flutterby." She lifted her eyebrows. "Yes?"

The woman was a little too perceptive. He sighed. "Maybe," he admitted reluctantly.

She cocked her head to one side. "You know, it's interesting to think about what your father would have thought of me, but I must confess I'm wondering what you think, Beau. Do you think I'm a flutterby?"

Beau was a straight shooter, but he would just as soon not answer her question. He lightly chucked her chin with his knuckles. "Too soon to know. It takes a while to determine the species."

"You don't trust me."

Her words were stark and blunt, unexpected. He frowned and shook his head. "I didn't say—"

"It's okay," she said, rubbing her cheek against his knuckles as if she were trying to soothe him and herself. Her eyes were vulnerable. "With the mistakes I've made lately, I'm not too sure I trust myself."

Beau's observation stabbed at Emily like a splinter. It made her wonder about herself. It forced her to re-evaluate her impulsive decision to make a temporary home in Ruxton. She began to ask herself questions, and she didn't have answers for all of them.

What was she doing here? Aside from the calamity

of her near-marriage, why didn't she have any desire to return to Roanoke? The only thing that nagged at her was the idea that she needed to settle unfinished business.

Her doubts troubled her. Although she understood Beau's reservation about her, she still felt frustrated by it because it stood between them. It was impossible to explain, futile to understand, but every emotional instinct she possessed pushed her closer to him. It was as if she was a river and he was the sea. Her heart allowed no choice. She had to go. In the back of her mind, though, she wondered where all this would lead.

"Where?" she muttered to herself as she joined Caroline for a stroll at the flea market. No sign of Beau today. His deputy was on duty while Beau took care of a crisis with some juvenile offenders.

"Where what?" Caroline said, gazing at Emily with dark eyes that resembled Beau's.

Emily bit her tongue. She hadn't realized she'd spoken aloud. "I wonder where Valene will set up the auction."

"Probably over by the weeping willow," Caroline said, pointing to a lush grassy patch in front of the tree. "Everyone's psyched about this services auction. I think the turnout will be great."

"I hope so," Emily said, picking up a tomato at the vegetable stand.

"I wonder if Beau will bring Donna." Caroline lowered her voice. "Nadine said she saw Donna corral him at the bar last night. She said Donna was all over him."

Emily felt an ugly twist in her stomach. Beau hadn't

visited her last night because she'd taken care of Hilary. He'd asked her to join him for the auction. It would be their first public appearance, but this morning he'd warned her the juvenile case might make him late. Emily's own doubts about their relationship roared to the surface. It required a major effort for her to make a noncommittal sound.

"Valene and I were talking about it the other day. We wish Beau would get involved with someone different. A woman who is decent and kind, who understands the importance of family and commitment."

Emily smiled weakly and mumbled again.

Caroline stepped closer to her. "Someone like you."

Alarm shot through her, and her thumb pierced the tomato skin. Emily paid for the bruised tomato and four almost ripe ones, then put them in her basket. "I think Beau prefers to make up his own mind."

"But you think he's attractive, don't you?"

"Well, of course, but—"

"There you go!" Caroline said in triumph.

"But I'm not inclined toward making any commitments right now," Emily quickly said.

"You will later," Caroline assured her. "And surely you can see that underneath his superior attitude, he's a wonderful man."

"I—uh—yes."

"There you go," Caroline said again. "You know what I like about you, Emily? You're such an honest, moral person without seeming like a goody-goody."

Emily wondered if this was when she should tell Caroline that just the other night she had nearly been begging Beau to take her on the hood of his car. "I'm glad you like me, but I'm not perfect by any means."

Caroline looked at her sideways and laughed. "Oh, you! Stop teasing me. What's the worse thing you've done? Go five miles over the speed limit?" Caroline shook her head. "If I've ever met someone as pure as the driven snow, Emily, it's you."

Emily sighed as Caroline walked ahead. "Slush," she muttered. "Pure as the driven slush."

Later that afternoon at the auction, Emily set her picnic basket on a blanket and watched the auctioneer fast-talk the bidders. As Beau had predicted, he was late. Glancing at her watch, she glumly began to wonder if he would show at all.

"Are you the new girl in town?" a woman's voice asked.

Emily glanced up and instantly recognized Beau's former lover. Her throat tensed, but she managed a smile. "Yes, I'm very new to Ruxton. And you?"

"Donna Grant," the woman said. "I'm a sales rep and I've lived here for a while. I'm hoping to be moved to a bigger territory soon." She smiled slightly. "They call you the five-minute bride. What's your real name?"

That pinched. *Who* called her the five-minute bride? "Emily St. Clair. It's a pleasure to meet you," she automatically said, thanking her lucky stars for being force-fed how to give polite responses at finishing school. She changed the subject away from herself. "The auction's a lot of fun, isn't it?"

Donna brushed a blade of grass from her jeans. "I guess so if you're into that sort of thing. I thought I might find Beau here. I asked around and people kept mentioning you. Was he supposed to meet you?''

How *direct,* Emily thought. "Yes, but he had some pressing work to do.''

Donna looked at her with an evaluating gaze. "I'm not going to beat around the bush. Beau and I've been involved, and I'd like to keep it that way.''

Emily wondered how in tarnation she was supposed to respond. She took a careful breath. "I'm not sure I can help you with that.''

"So he's started seeing you," she said, her voice hinting at all kinds of conclusions. "You and he have an arrangement.''

Her stomach clenched. "I—I—don't think I would call it an arrangement. We haven't known each other very long," Emily managed to say, then stood. "Oh, look. They're starting the bidding on the window-cleaning service. I wanted to try for that one. Please excuse me," she said in a rush. "It was nice meeting you.''

Emily escaped the other woman's presence, but she couldn't avoid the word *arrangement* as it echoed inside her mind over and over again. She won the bid for the window cleaners and confirmed her purchase at the registration table. Her head began to throb with tension and she strongly considered leaving, but Beau came up behind her.

"Shopping again?" he teased, putting his arm around her waist.

She managed a smile. "I like the idea of someone else doing my second-story windows.''

"Thought you wanted to try all the things you've never tried before," he murmured close to her ear.

A pleasurable shudder ran through her. "Try the things I've always *wanted* to try," she corrected.

"Where do I fit in all of that?"

"You can be trying," she told him, and laughed at his scowl. She met his gaze and lowered her voice. "There are more things I'd like to try with you."

Squeezing her waist, he looked at her with sensual promise in his dark eyes. "Then you will."

His expression was so intense it made her feel hot and restless. She looked away and took a quick breath. "How did your juvenile case turn out?"

Beau shook his head. "The kid's in a tough situation, but this is the second car he's hot-wired and stolen. When I talked to the D.A., I made noises about wanting stronger efforts for rehabilitation so this boy doesn't become an adult offender. Juvenile cases always require an incredible amount of time and paperwork." He brushed his hand through his hair in exasperation. "I've had enough of it today. When's your computer-service offer coming up for bid?"

Emily cocked her head and listened to the auctioneer. "I think they're announcing it now. Did I tell you I received three phone calls from small local businesses asking me to consult on a part-time basis?" She felt a rush of excitement. "Right now it's mostly moonlighting, but it could grow. Who would have ever thought Emily could become an entrepreneur?"

"An underestimated woman," Beau said wryly, "can be very dangerous. And, darlin', you have been grossly underestimated."

"By whom?"

"By just about everyone, including you." The bidding began, and he narrowed his gaze. "Why the hell is Hank bidding? He wouldn't know what to do with a computer if it bit him," he muttered.

"All the more reason for him to become educated."

Beau looked down his nose at Emily. "By whom?"

She smiled. "By *me* if he wins the bid."

Beau frowned.

Emily watched the bidding rise to fifty dollars and tried unsuccessfully not to think about her earlier conversation with Donna. *You have an arrangement.* She didn't like the way that statement felt. It sounded controlled and businesslike, when she felt emotional and out of control. It didn't sit right with her, but she wondered if it was the truth, at least for Beau.

"Going, going—"

Beau lifted his hand and shouted, "Fifty-five!"

She blinked and watched in amazement as Hank and Beau drove the bidding higher. When they hit seventy-five dollars, she tugged on Beau's sleeve. "Why are you bidding on this when you can get it free?"

He chuckled. "I'm glad you're offering your services *free* for me, but I don't trust Hank's motives."

She opened her mouth to correct him, but he called out another bid. The county would pay for her services to Beau's office. It took her a moment to understand what he'd said about Hank. She couldn't believe this was some sort of macho competitive game over her! When the light dawned, she stifled a groan. "This is insanity," she said, and walked away.

"Emily," he called after her. "Emily," he said again, but she just kept on walking.

Not more than a minute later, Beau was jogging to catch up with her. "Hold on. Why'd you leave?"

"I'm confused. First you act like you think I'm about as substantial as cotton candy, then you give me the rush. You indicate you don't want everyone to know we're involved. You're not interested in commitment. Then you get into a bidding war with Hank over two hours of computer time with me."

He shrugged. "Things change."

His response failed to satisfy her. "Maybe," she thought, and continued walking.

Beau put out his arm to stop her. "What's with you tonight?"

Emily tensed. She didn't want to explain herself. She wasn't certain she understood everything herself. "I don't know," she said. "I've just been thinking a lot this afternoon."

"About what?" he demanded.

"About a lot of things," she said, then changed the subject. "Are you hungry? I think I'd like to eat. I've set up a blanket there," she told him, pointing toward the picnic area.

He hesitated, then nodded. "Okay. We can talk later."

Emily wasn't looking forward to it.

As the evening progressed, Beau noticed Emily seemed more withdrawn than usual. Even when his sisters came by to rib him, Emily was polite, but quiet. By the time they left the auction, he was compelled to learn what was bothering her. He didn't completely understand his drive. In normal circumstances, he wouldn't want to know too much about why a woman wasn't talking, because it usually meant she wanted something from him that he couldn't give.

He brought his truck to a stop outside his house and watched her. She was a crazy combination of women in one, he thought. Pretty, but proper on the outside, polite, impertinent, playful on the inside. As a lover, she was a damn fast learner. Her unguarded expressiveness kept him wanting more.

Even now he wanted to be touching her, but tonight she seemed remote. "What brought on all this thinking?"

She slid a sideways gaze at him. "You say that as if thinking is a bad thing."

"No," he said, carefully considering his next response. "Thinking is good as long as you don't get off on the wrong track. But you didn't really answer my question. What brought it on?"

She rolled down her window. "I met Donna Grant tonight."

Beau rubbed his chin and sighed. This could get messy. "Donna and I were—" He paused, trying to find the right description for a relationship that had involved his body, but never his heart. "We had an arrangement."

"I know. Your sisters told me. Donna told me." She paused. "When people get involved, unfortunately there is sometimes a difference in the intensity of their emotions."

"What are you saying?"

"Donna wants to continue your arrangement."

Beau frowned. "I've been over this with her. I don't know why she dragged you into it."

"It was a brief conversation. She was curious."

Impatience licked through him. "About what?"

"You and me," Emily said, still looking out the window. "She wanted to know if you and I had an arrangement."

"What did you say?"

"I said I wouldn't choose that term. It sounds cold to me." She finally turned to look at him. "I wondered what term you would choose."

Irritated with Donna's interference, Beau swore under his breath. "It's not the same as it was with her."

"That's good to know," she said politely, and he could see she was struggling with it. "Just out of curiosity, how would you describe us?"

Crazy. Intimate. Unexpected friends. Unplanned lovers. All those descriptions made him uncomfortable. He went for something more rational. "I would say we have an understanding."

She nodded, but he wanted to close the distance he saw in her eyes immediately.

"What do you think?"

"It doesn't reveal anything about your feelings," she told him as she opened her door. "It's noncommittal, which is consistent. I think it sounds sleazy," she finished saying, in a crisp, prissy voice.

And Beau knew by the way she slammed her door when she got out of his truck that he'd really blown it this time.

Ten

"**W**ell, hell!"

Emily felt Beau overtake her quick stride. She stiffly came to a stop. She felt stiff and tense. She felt confused.

"How should I explain our relationship?" he demanded. "You want me to say we're lovers?"

She blinked, taken aback. "I—"

"I could tell people to mind their own damn business," he offered.

"Well, you—"

"Or do you want me to tell them how I really *feel?*" He said the 'F' word with true masculine distaste. "That I want to lock you up in my house and make love to you until we physically can't lift a finger. That I want to punch Hank for looking at you twice. That you've affected me like no other woman has, and

I'd like you to stay around a lot longer than I think you're going to. As much as you say you're staying in Ruxton, I know you're going back to Roanoke."

Emily simply stared at him. His words rattled inside her head like pinballs in a machine, bouncing off emotionally loaded areas inside her. Her knees felt weak. She hadn't realized that the intensity of his feelings mirrored her own. "Give me a minute," she said.

Beau stepped closer, his eyes darkly passionate. "Sometimes I feel like I don't have a minute. Sometimes I'm sure I'm going to turn around and in a flash you'll be gone. My saner half tells me to pull back. Then some other part I didn't even know existed keeps pushing me closer to you. You wanna tell me how the hell to explain that to the folks in town?"

Distress crowded her throat. She identified with much of what he was saying. She wished she knew herself better. A sound of frustration escaped her mouth. "For a twenty-five year old, I feel like I should have a much better grasp on who I am and what I want. But I don't. I'm so afraid of making another mess of my life. I don't want to mess up yours, either. You don't trust me, and maybe you shouldn't. I told you I'm not sure I trust myself right now."

She grabbed her courage in her hand and continued, searching his eyes. "But, Beau, I've never met anyone like you, and I just don't want to find myself missing you someday. Ready or not, I don't want to ever miss you."

He looked away and swore. "The timing sucks."

Her heart contracted. "So what do we do?"

He looked back at her, and she watched something

shift in his eyes. From doubt and caution to passionate abandon, it was like watching a rider let out the reins on his horse.

Emily felt a wave of anticipation rush through her, and her own doubts seemed to take flight.

"I think it's time we stop *counting* the minutes and start living them," he told her in a deep voice that sent a shudder through her. "You game?"

It was a risky venture, she knew, and she wouldn't be able to protect her heart. All or nothing. It frightened her, but that same need pounded through her. "Yes," she whispered.

He swung her up in his arms and headed for the house.

Emily struggled for a breath. "What are you doing?"

"We made a deal. No use in wasting time," he told her, and pushed open his front door.

"Guess not," she murmured, certain she'd left half her mind in his driveway.

Beau strode through his den, past his black Lab Cookie, to his bedroom. Setting her down next to his nightstand, he wrapped his hand around the nape of her neck and took her mouth in a hungry kiss.

The room began to swim, and she clung to his shoulders. When she was certain she was going to melt into one of the cracks in his hardwood floor, he pulled away. She had to lock her knees to keep from pitching toward him.

If she'd been unsure of his plans before, she knew without a doubt what he intended when he pulled a handful of condoms out of the drawer, tore one open and put it on top of the nightstand.

"I have got to have you," he said.

His intensity almost made her nervous. He didn't wear a gentle look on his face or an easy expression in his eyes. Undiluted need. It gave her a rush. When had she been needed like this? A strange sense of power rushed through her.

"Then take me," she said, leaning into him and lifting her mouth to his. "And let me take you."

Tumbling backward on the bed, Beau pulled her with him, catching her against him. He slid his hands beneath her skirt and skimmed them up her thighs to her bottom to rock her pelvis against his. "You have on too many clothes."

His heat cranked up her body temperature, his need spurred her own. "No more than you," she managed to say.

He slipped one of his hands up her blouse and released a few of the buttons to cup one of her lace-covered breasts. He smiled. "I'm not wearing a bra."

Emily's mouth went dry when his thumb flicked across her nipple. She couldn't muster a grin. "I'm not wearing socks."

"Oh, Emily," he groaned, and undid the catch of her bra.

She tugged his shirt free and ran her hands over the hard planes of his chest and abdomen. He sucked in his belly when her fingers trailed just beneath his waistband. He arched his hips against her, and she felt the thrust of his hard masculinity beneath his jeans.

The knowledge of his arousal turned her on even

more. She slid her fingertips over his nipples, caught between her desire to go wild with his body or to wait for him.

He put his hand over hers and let her continue stroking him. "What is it?"

"You make me want to do all kinds of things to your body, Beau." She lightly squeezed his nipples and rolled her lower body against his.

He closed his eyes for a second and swore. "What kinds of things?"

"I want to lick—" she began, taking a breath. "You."

He groaned again. "Where?"

Emily looked at his body and felt shamelessly hungry. His chest was a work of art, beautifully carved pectorals with a dusting of hair that arrowed down to his flat belly. He was so strong, and his inner and outer strength was incredibly sexy to her. "Everywhere," she admitted.

"Oh, Lord, what are you waiting for?"

"To see if it's okay with you."

He rolled his head from side to side. "Are you gonna make me beg?"

Emily smiled. "Could I?"

He glanced at her through slitted eyes looking like a hungry lion. "Show a little mercy, devil woman. Payback's hell."

Leaning forward, she skimmed her tongue over his throat and slid her hands down to unfasten his waistband. "I like this perspective," she murmured.

"You like being on top," he said in a wry, but husky voice.

Scooting back slightly, she eased his zipper down. "Well, I've never really—"

He brushed aside her bra. "You've never done a lot of things."

"I'm trying to amend that," she said, feeling both determined and hot. She lowered her head to his chest and licked his nipples the same way he'd licked her. He arched beneath her, and she was awed again at the power and strength of his body.

Rubbing openmouthed kisses over his chest and upper abdomen, she slid her hand inside his loosened jeans and touched him.

He jerked.

"Do you want me to stop?"

"No, no, no." He rolled her nipples between his thumb and forefinger.

The mesmerizing little caress distracted her, made her restless. She rubbed her hair back and forth against his belly, and felt him stiffen as if he were struggling to control himself.

Inhaling deeply, Emily felt the need to be closer to him grow wider and deeper inside her. It seemed to stretch her and take up every available corner. In her heart. In her mind. In her body. She wondered why she loved the way he smelled, why the texture of his skin fascinated her, why she wanted to taste him so badly. She wondered why she wanted to be what he needed in a woman whatever that was. So many depended on him, but she wanted to be someone he could depend on.

Close enough, intimate enough, just didn't seem to exist. Her desire to pleasure him was endless. She stroked his hardened masculinity again and met his gaze. His eyes were nearly black with arousal, his nostrils flared.

"Come here, sweetheart. I want to kiss you."

Her heart pounded against her rib cage. In all her life, she'd never really been anyone's sweetheart. Not like this. Taking a quick breath, she shook her head. "Not yet," she told him and rode the wave of her instincts. "I might not do this right," she whispered, pushing aside a sliver of uncertainty, as she took him into her mouth.

He was satin and steel against her lips, and she tasted him again and again. She rolled her tongue over the tip of his arousal and was surprised that pleasuring him was such a turn-on. His shudder vibrated inside her. Swollen with wanting him, she continued until he slipped his fingers through her hair and urged her head up.

"I'm on the edge," he said roughly.

"That's okay," she told him and tried to lower her mouth again.

"No. Oh, help me." He sucked in a deep breath of air. "Not this way, not this time," he murmured as much to himself as to her and dragged her up his body. "What am I going to do with you, Emily?"

The hopeless note in his voice wrenched at her. "Let me make love to you this time. Let me."

"But—"

"Let me," she repeated and kissed him. A second passed and he lost it, taking her mouth as if he couldn't get enough of her. Distantly, she felt him pull her skirt up and push her panties down. His fingers searched and found her wet with wanting. He made the ache worse by caressing her, sliding his finger just inside her.

She strained against him, her breaths matching his. With trembling fingers she reached for the protection on the nightstand and fumbled as she put it on him. Her mind a haze of arousal, she shook her head. "I need to take off this skirt."

Beau shook his head and wrapped his hands around her waist, drawing her above him. "Just sit," he told her, rubbing his masculinity at her entrance.

Swallowing hard, she vacillated. They were both still partly clothed, but the urgency between them was overwhelming. Trapped in his gaze, she eased, inch by inch down on him until he filled her.

He closed his eyes for a moment, relishing the intimate moment, then opened them. Emily felt his gaze of approval on her as he released one of her wrists and slipped his fingers between them. She had never felt so voluptuous in her life. She had never known she could.

He fondled her sensitive femininity, making her undulate.

"Oh, yes," he said. "Grab my shoulders, Emily."

She leaned forward needed something to brace herself on.

"Ride me," he told her, moving inside her at a slow, mind-bending rhythm.

Emily followed her heart again. He led. She followed. Then she led, and he followed. In the end he took her mind, body and soul, but Emily saw the reality on his face, and it rocked her foundations. She had taken him, too.

For a few minutes they dozed together. Beau felt her wiggle and tightened his arms.

"I need to visit your bathroom," she murmured.

He allowed her to go, opening his eyes enough to catch sight of her beautiful backside as she slipped out of bed. Lifting his hand to his forehead, he covered his eyes and wondered how he'd gotten into this. He'd never been one to cling to anyone. After living in a houseful of women, being alone and having his privacy had seemed like a gift. Now it was as if Emily had walked into his life and shown him this huge empty hole in his life that only she could fill.

Beau found that notion enormously disturbing because his instincts warned him that she wouldn't stay. Even if he asked her to stay.

She breezed back into the bedroom, interrupting his dark thoughts. He chuckled, suspecting she moved so quickly because she was unaccustomed to being watched while she walked around in the nude. Just as she slipped into bed and pulled up the sheet, she stopped, staring into the open bedside drawer.

She turned to him curiously. "What's in this drawer?"

"What?"

"It looks like buckles. Belt buckles."

"Oh, yeah," he said. "Those are some of the buckles I won during my rodeo days. I stuffed them in the drawer till I could figure out what to do with them."

She looked at him in disbelief. "For two years?"

He shrugged.

She pulled one out of the drawer. "You should display them."

Beau got a kick out of her fascination with his awards. "Uh-oh," he said. "I never would have thought you'd be a buckle bunny."

Her eyebrows wrinkled in confusion. "Buckle bunny?"

Leaning closer, he pulled her to him. "A buckle bunny is a woman who chases the rodeo winners."

She cocked her head to one side thoughtfully. "And this woman has a fixation with—" She met his gaze. "Buckles."

Beau bit back his amusement. "You could say that."

She peeked back into his drawer, then looked back at him, her expression rife with speculation. "You have a *lot* of buckles. Big buckles."

Beau roared with laughter and squeezed her against him again.

When he quieted down, he watched her run her fingers over his buckle. "Did you wear a costume and a hat? Do you ever wear the buckles? Did you have boots? What kind of horses did you—"

"Hold on, Miss Curious. I had a couple of fancy shirts I wore, and yeah, I wore a black hat and boots. The horses—"

"A black hat?" she repeated with excitement.

"Yes."

"When I was little, I wanted to be a cowboy with a black hat."

"A cowgirl," he corrected.

She shook her head. "No. On TV, the cowboys always got to do the fun stuff. I never saw any cowgirls wearing black hats."

Beau took in the sight of her for a long moment, angelic blond hair, fair skin and wide blue eyes. Beneath that classy, demure outer covering lay a gambler's heart. Who would have thought it? Who would have known? The man who won her would need that information, Beau thought. The man who hoped to keep her would need to understand the polite exterior and appreciate the untamed, adventurous part of her.

Beau wasn't sure he was the man who would ultimately win her and keep her, but he could give her this little fantasy. Keeping his odd mix of amusement and more intense emotions to himself, he rolled out of bed and pulled on his jeans.

Emily pulled the sheet farther up her chest. "What are you doing?"

"Just a minute," he said. He thumbed through some clothes in his closet until he found one of his old rodeo shirts, and tossed it toward her.

"What's this?"

"Just a minute," he said again, and grabbed his black hat from the shelf in the closet. He threw that on the bed too. Then he found a belt with one of the rodeo buckles hanging from a nail, snatched his boots from the closet floor, and strolled toward her.

She was already inspecting the hat in her hand, then she glanced up at him doubtfully. "You don't really think I'm going to—"

"First things first." Beau cracked a smile. "Lift your arms."

She kept playing with the hat, but her expression was self-conscious. "This isn't necessary. The cowboy fantasy was a long time ago. Right after the princess fantasy and before the motorcycle fantasy."

"Are you saying you don't *secretly* still want to dress up like a cowboy?"

Her cheeks flamed, and she lifted her chin. "I didn't say that. I just—" She broke off, looked at the hat, then back at him. "This is crazy."

"Lift your arms," he told her.

She hesitated briefly, then dropped the sheet.

Beau looked at her breasts and felt the punch of want in his midsection. He swore. "It's a shame to cover your body, but—" He pulled the shirt up her arms, and they both worked on the buttons.

She looked at him curiously. "This is the second time you've dressed me."

"Yeah." He pulled the belt around her and put it on the tightest loop, but it still almost fell off her hips.

"Is this some kind of unusual fetish?"

Beau laughed. "Are you worried that I secretly played with my sisters' Barbie dolls when I was a kid and I miss changing doll clothes?"

Her lips twitched. "Did you?"

"You've found out my secret. I did get into my sisters' Barbie dolls." He caught sight of her widened eyes. "I liked taking their heads off and hiding them."

Emily rolled her eyes and sighed. "You're terrible."

"That's me. Step into the boots, wild woman."

"I'm not wild," she protested, but put her feet in the boots and stood.

He put the hat on the back of her head because it was a little too big for her, then tightened the cord under her chin.

"This is ridiculous," she muttered.

Beau tugged her toward the full-length mirror on the back of his closet door.

"This is crazy," she grumbled, nearly tripping because the boots were way too big. "I'm not a child. I don't go to sleep every night wishing for a horse named Black Devil anymore, or one of those fringy jackets or—"

She looked at the mirror and stopped. Beau watched her face light up like a Christmas tree and felt the oddest, most painful tugging sensation in his chest. He shoved his hands in his pockets to keep from reaching for her.

Her eyes met his in the mirror and she beamed. "I love the hat."

"You can keep it," he told her. He suspected she'd be taking a helluva lot more from him than his hat when she left.

Aghast, she whirled around to face him. "Oh, no! This is an important memento from your rodeo days."

"Nah. I like the way it looks on you." When she started to protest, he frowned. "You'll hurt my feelings if you don't take it."

She hesitated, then laughed. "Why do I think that's a slight exaggeration?"

"Beats me. I'm just an honest, sensitive, nice guy."

She laughed harder.

Moving closer to her, he ran his gaze down her full length and shook his head. The black shirt sparkled with studs and beads, and the fringe rippled when her breasts bounced. It stopped mid-thigh, revealing her pale, shapely legs. "I tell you one thing. The shirt never looked that good on me."

"I'm sure that's a matter of opinion," she said, her hands on her hips. "Buckle bunnies?" she prompted.

Beau chewed the inside of his lip to keep from chuckling at her curiosity. "I can't remember."

"I'm disappointed," she said with a mock innocent expression on her face.

"Why?"

"I was hoping you'd tell me what buckle bunnies did." She lifted her arms around his neck.

Beau felt his body begin to heat again. He knew what was underneath her shirt. He knew how good she felt beneath him. "The other guys talked sometimes. I might be able to remember some of the things they told me." He pulled his hands from his pockets and wrapped his arms around her. "It might take a little encouragement."

She gave a little smile and lifted on tiptoe to press her lips to his. "How's this?"

"Good for a start." He lifted her high in his arms and one of the boots fell to the floor. She was taking him by inches, he realized. Taking little bits of his mind, body and soul. A slow and easy invasion, as if she could never threaten his life-style or sanity. It felt like heaven, but a part of him wondered when it would turn to hell.

Eleven

"**Y**ou still haven't let me light your cigar," Emily told Beau as she watched him take a discreet puff on her front porch several days later. It intrigued her that he was so selective about when he smoked in front of her. He was getting ready to leave for a meeting, and it was silly, but she would miss him.

"It's self-protection," he said with an intimate half grin that brought to mind all the pleasures they'd shared. "I'm afraid you'll set me on fire."

"Oh, you're so clever." She bit her lip to keep from laughing. He made her feel light and easy, wanted and wanting. She lifted her hand to his arm, then pulled back.

The afternoon sun played over his hard features. He arched an eyebrow. "Why'd you stop?"

"It just feels so natural to touch you, and I have to

keep reminding myself that you might not be a 'toucher.'''

He sifted his fingers though her hair and gently kissed her forehead. ''It feels natural for me to touch you, too. So don't stop on my account.''

Emily rested her cheek against his chest where his heart beat. Why did it always feel so right to be with him? Why was it that all she had to do to want him more was listen to him talk about everyday matters? And yet, logically, she knew it was too soon.

She closed her eyes against logic for a second. ''What kind of turnout do you think you'll get tonight for the Big Buddy program?''

''I'm hoping for twenty men. Then that twenty can do some arm twisting and bring in twenty more.''

Emily admired Beau for using his influence to make a difference among the youth of the town. ''If you weren't focusing on male volunteers, I would be happy to come.''

''I appreciate it, but you would distract them.''

She sighed. ''You overestimate my—''

The sound of a vehicle coming to a screeching halt in front of Emily's house grabbed their attention.

''Who in hell—'' Beau began.

''Who is—''

Emily blinked, then recognized the two occupants of the green convertible. ''Maddie! Jenna!'' She grabbed Beau's hand and dragged him with her down the steps. ''They're my two best friends in the world. Bridesmaids in my wedd—'' She made a face. ''Well, my almost-wedding.''

Red-haired Maddie swung out of the car, heedless

of the wild state of her bob, and practically skipped up the walk. "Surprise!" she called.

Jenna tugged ineffectually to get her brown hair back into place and wore a put-upon look. "Hi, Em. I wanted to call, but Maddie insisted."

"No problem. It's great to see you both." She hugged her friends.

"I thought you'd be languishing here in Podunk, North Carolina," Maddie said, lifting her big sunglasses to peer at Emily. "But you look plenty healthy to me."

"I like Ruxton," Emily told her. "Let me introduce you. This is Beau Ramsey. He's the local—"

"He looks a lot like the officer who stopped me on the interstate about an hour ago." Maddie shook her head in disgust. "Amazing how crabby these lawman types get when you're ten miles over the speed limit."

"It was eighteen," Jenna corrected, "but I talked him down to five. You've got a lead foot." She extended her hand toward Beau. "It's nice to meet you, and something makes me think Maddie just stepped in it again. Do you have some relationship with law enforcement?"

"I'm the sheriff."

"Oh." Maddie let out a squeak of dismay.

"How did you know?" he asked.

Jenna shrugged. "Professional instinct. I'm assistant Commonwealth Attorney in Roanoke."

"Why don't we go inside and I'll get us something to drink?" Emily offered.

As if he knew another couple of tornadoes had

rolled into his town, Beau shook his head. "You'll have to excuse me. I've got a meeting."

Emily searched his face, but found it unreadable. "Are you sure you can't stay for a few minutes?"

"I've gotta go."

"Just a minute," she said to Maddie and Jenna and walked with Beau to his truck. "Will you come by after the meeting?"

"It'll be late."

Emily frowned. She wondered why he suddenly seemed distant. "Will you call?"

He met her gaze. "You'll be busy with your friends."

She wished his eyes weren't quite so calm and cool. Her chest grew tight with apprehension, and she withdrew, too. "Okay. Thank you for lunch," she managed politely.

"I'll be in touch," he said, then got in his truck. "You might tell your friend she's parked facing the wrong direction. I'd hate to see her get two tickets in one day."

"Thanks," Emily said, but he was already backing out of her driveway. She wondered why the sudden change in his mood. He'd been so warm, and then it was as if he couldn't get away fast enough.

Glancing at her friends on the porch, she shook her head and decided to think about it later. It wasn't often Maddie and Jenna showed up on her doorstep.

Within two hours, Maddie had managed to coax them into going to a honky-tonk in a neighboring town.

"We thought we'd find you depressed and in seclusion," Maddie said once they were seated and had drinks before them. "But you're blooming. What gives?"

Emily smiled. "You'll probably think I'm crazy, but I believe calling off my wedding was the best thing that could have happened to me."

"You do look happy," Jenna said. "Anything to do with the sheriff?"

"Great eye candy," Maddie added, then scrunched up her face. "But did you have to pick a sheriff? They make me nervous."

"If you would obey the laws," Jenna told her, "you wouldn't have a problem."

"I obey them ninety-nine percent of the time and nobody notices. It's the one percent that kills me. I color outside the lines just a little bit and I always get caught. It must be my destiny," she muttered darkly, and took a sip of her beer.

"The original question was directed to you, Emily," Jenna prompted. "How serious are you about the sheriff?"

Very. She swallowed the immediate response and ignored the tight feeling in her midsection. She shouldn't be, couldn't be... "It's too soon to say." She said the appropriate words, but they didn't ring true. Impatient with herself, she gave up fighting the truth. "I'm in love with him."

Maddie's eyes rounded.

Jenna simply nodded. "Rebound?"

"Honest?" Emily asked. "I don't think so. But I'm going through a lot of changes right now, so I'd like some time to be sure."

"What's the sheriff's story?"

"I think he doesn't trust me." It hurt to say it, more than she'd realized.

Maddie looked offended. "Doesn't trust *you?* Your middle name is dependable."

"Was," Emily corrected. "Since I came to Ruxton, I've reassessed things. I've been trying things I always wanted to try, like horseback riding. I worked in a bar, then found a temp computer job with the county. I'm starting to do computer consultations on the side, and it could conceivably build into a self-supporting business. I rented a house, and I like it here. No one knows me, so they don't expect me to be the way I was in Roanoke. For the first time in years, I feel like I can breathe."

"Your mother *can* be stifling," Jenna said.

Out of habit Emily opened her mouth to defend her mother, but she stopped before she spoke. Jenna was right. "Yes, she can."

"Now *she* has been in seclusion," Maddie said. "None of her friends have seen hide nor hair of her."

Emily winced. "I had hoped she would have started to get over it by now."

"I imagine she still feels embarrassed," Jenna said.

"Embarrassed!" Maddie said. "Try totally humiliated. She was counting on this being 'the wedding of the century.' A bunch of people think you must be crushed, because you moved away."

Emily frowned. "I'm not sure I care all that much what they're saying at the country club about me, but I really couldn't be less crushed."

"We can see that," Jenna told her.

Emily waited to hear more. "I hear a *but*."

"I'm not suggesting that you should give a rip what the country club set thinks. It looks as if you're thriving here." Jenna gave a wry smile. "As much as I'd like you to come back, you're happier than I've seen you in a long time."

Emily smiled. "You're not in court, Jenna. I still hear a *but*."

"I wonder if it might help resolve things for you and your mom if you paid a quick visit. A quick *visible* visit."

Sighing, Emily pondered her friend's suggestion. "I hate the idea of people pitying me."

Maddie shrugged. "Tell them to suck eggs and die."

Emily laughed.

Jenna grinned. "Not a bad idea. But if that doesn't work, you could just tell them the truth."

Emily considered what Maddie and Jenna had said. The more she thought about it, the more she knew she needed to pay a visit to her mother. "What time do you think we should leave in the morning?"

Jenna and Maddie spoke at once.

"Eight a.m."

"Eleven o'clock."

Maddie looked appalled. "Eight a.m. on a Saturday morning? Are you a sadist?"

"She'll need to get to the country club by lunchtime," Jenna said, then her lips twitched. "I'll drive. You can sleep."

"Well if Emily's gotta face her mother tomorrow, the least we can do is give her a good time tonight."

Well acquainted with Maddie's concept of a good time, Emily shook her head. Visions of tabletop dancing, too much liquor and police raids danced in her head. "That's not necessary," she said. "A good night's sleep will do me a—"

"I want that one," Maddie said, snagging a waiter. She pointed to a tall man standing alone at the bar. She gave the waiter a few dollars. "My friend would like to buy him a beer. Tell him she's blond."

Emily felt her cheeks heat.

"She means well," Jenna said sympathetically.

When the man at the bar walked toward her with a big grin, she moaned. "Maddie did you have to do this?"

"Don't thank me," she mocked, then snagged another waiter. She pressed a couple of bucks into his palm. "My friend would like to buy that man a drink. Tell him she's brunette."

Jenna choked on her drink and gaped at Maddie.

"She means well," Emily whispered.

Jenna narrowed her eyes. "Maybe so, but she's paying for this one."

After Emily dragged herself out of bed the next morning and showered, she immediately called Beau.

"H'lo."

His rumbly voice made her smile. She could easily imagine waking up to him every day. Her heart squeezed. "Good morning. This is Emily."

A long pause followed, and she almost wondered if he'd fallen asleep. "Beau?"

"Late night last night?"

Emily laughed lightly. "Maddie. We practically had to drag her out of The Cherry Bomb. She was determined that Jenna and I have a good time. She thinks we don't get out enough and—" Emily stopped. "Did I miss you last night? Did you stop by after all?"

"No big deal," he said. "I drove by after the meeting."

Something about his tone didn't sound right. "Darn. I wish I'd seen you. Especially now." She took a deep breath. "Jenna and Maddie talked with me, and I think I should make a quick trip back to Roanoke. I'm only planning to stay overnight," she emphasized.

When he didn't say anything, she continued. "I'm not looking forward to it, but I think it's the right thing to do."

"When are you leaving?" His voice was expressionless.

She frowned. "In just a few minutes, but I'll be back tomorrow because I have to work on Monday."

"You want me to tell your landlord for you?" Beau asked.

"Why?" she asked, totally confused. "It's just for one night."

He gave a heavy sigh. "It's easy for one night to turn into two," he told her. "I always knew you'd go back. This was just sooner than I expected."

Frustrated, she crammed her feet into her shoes and began to pace around her bedroom. "This is *one* night," she insisted. "I'll be back tomorrow."

"If you say so," he said, his voice full of disbelief.

"I do. Can we see each other when I get back?"

"Sure," he said, without an ounce of commitment.

"Why don't you believe me?"

He paused a long moment, and his silence hurt her. "Butterfly, flutterby," he said quietly.

His words hurt worse. She wished he believed in her half as much as she believed in him. Fighting the stinging sensation in her eyes, she swallowed over her crowded throat. "I guess you'll just have to see."

"Emily," he said. "Take care of yourself."

This was ridiculous, she thought. "Thank you. I will," she said, switching to her controlled polite mode.

"And if you ever light a man's cigar," he told her with a forced chuckle, "use hickory matches."

Anger, hot and intense, raced through her, burning a hole in her polite control, and Emily did something she'd never done before. She hung up on him.

If one more person asked him about Emily, he was going to punch them. He'd joined his sisters for dinner in hopes of avoiding the too-quiet loneliness of his home. His sisters, however, had each privately grilled him about Emily. He felt as if he'd been poked and prodded by far too many people.

Beau had always figured a sore heart could be cured with a good bottle of whiskey or a great meal or another woman, but he was sadly mistaken.

He resented Emily for blowing into town and turning every man on his ear including him. He resented her because he used to enjoy the quiet solitude of his home. He resented her because he hadn't known there'd been an empty place in his life that only she could fill. He resented her for the laughter and light she'd brought him, because now everything seemed dark and sad.

He wished she'd never come to Ruxton. He wished he'd never made love to her. He wished he'd never fallen in love with her.

Feeling a tug on his pants leg, he glanced down to see Hilary Bell looking up at him. His sisters had invited her and her mother for dinner. He patted her on the head. "How ya' doing, sweetheart?"

"I miss Miss Emily," she said with a big sigh.

Beau felt his chest tighten painfully. Lord, the woman had launched a full-scale invasion and they'd all been helpless against it. Beau patted her again. "Me, too, darlin'. Me, too."

As soon as Marie opened the door to her mother and stepfather's expansive home in Hunting Hills, Emily breezed past the housekeeper with a smile. "Is she in the Florida room or in the bedroom with the curtains drawn?"

"Her bedroom, but—"

Emily made a face. "That bad, huh? I'll go up now."

The housekeeper trotted after her. "I think it might be best if I announce you."

"Oh, no. It sounds like she could use a little shock treatment."

Marie frowned. "I don't know…"

But Emily was already up the winding staircase. She walked down the long hallway to her mother's closed bedroom door and heard the hum of Saturday morning television. *This was bad.* Her mother didn't often give in to full-scale melodrama, but it appeared she'd pulled out all the stops this time.

Bracing herself, she tapped on the door.

"Come in, Marie."

Emily pushed open the door and saw her mother in a rose chiffon negligee and dressing gown reclining on the bed with the remote control, her pocket poodle and a pitcher of Mimosa on the nightstand.

"Good morning, Mother," Emily said, and glanced at the television. "I always thought professional wrestling was an oxymoron."

Adrian St. Clair Bennet's eyes briefly widened in surprise before she regained her composure. Her mother was the queen of composure. "I'm tired of 'Power Rangers.'"

"Then join me for lunch," Emily said, marveling again at her mother's natural beauty. She'd often felt gangly and inferior around her mother. It wasn't hard to imagine why.

"Ralph already invited me."

Emily thought of her filthy-rich stepfather with a heart of gold and smiled. "Where is he?"

Her mother gave a wounded look. "Golfing."

Emily nodded and moved closer to sit on the edge of the bed. "You feel abandoned."

"I can't imagine why," she said. "First, my daughter walks out during the middle of her wedding and literally runs away. Then my husband goes golfing."

"Mom, I can't say I'm sorry for stopping the wedding or even for running away. It would have been wrong for me to marry Carl. I can say I'm sorry this has been so embarrassing for you. You don't deserve it."

Her mother lifted her chin and gave Emily a considering glance. "You've changed."

Emily smiled. "I hope so."

"You need a haircut."

Emily bit back her amusement. "Possibly."

"Are you wearing *any* cosmetics at all?"

"Not much makeup today. I was in a rush to see my mom."

Affection stole into her mother's eyes. "Where did you want to go to lunch, dear?"

"The country club," Emily said, surprised her mother would need to ask. "We have reservations in thirty minutes."

Her mother looked doubtful. "Oh, I don't know."

"People think you're languishing in humiliation, and they think I'm *scared* to show my face in public. To quote Maddie, you've been indisposed long enough. It's time to strut your stuff and give the old bags an eyeful."

Her mother's mouth twitched. "I always thought that with some work, some serious work," her mother added as she gracefully rose from the bed, "your friend Maddie would be a force to reckon with."

Emily laughed. "I think she already is."

Thirty minutes later Emily and her mother walked into the Hunting Hills Country Club. The dining room possessed friendly waiters, good food and an understated elegance. Deep green carpet adorned with a rose-colored floral pattern cushioned the feet of the well-heeled members. The dining room chairs were upholstered in rose, and sterling silver clinked against gold-rimmed ivory china on tables decked in white cloths. The most impressive features of the room, however, were the two walls of large-pane windows and the wealth of its occupants.

Emily's mother picked at her hearts of palm salad while Emily finished the last bite of her cantaloupe. Odd, she thought. She couldn't remember a time when her mother had been more ill at ease.

"I think I'm becoming an entrepreneur," Emily said. "I'm a computer consultant."

Adrian smiled. "I'll have to tell Ralph. He'll be so impressed." She dabbed at the corner of her mouth. "I must tell you I don't blame you for walking out on Carl. Even though he was a doctor, he didn't deserve you."

"Thank you," Emily said, and took a sip of water. "I agree."

Adrian chuckled lightly, then sighed. "You remind me of your father more and more, darling. With each passing day."

Emily resisted the urge to make sure her hair was covering her ears. "Is it my ears?"

"I wasn't thinking of your ears. I was thinking of your independence and sense of humor. Oh, how that man could make me laugh, even during a rough moment."

"Do you feel the same way about Ralph?"

Adrian gave a sad smile. "I love Ralph in a different way. He has given me security and peace. Your father gave me laughter and passion."

Emily felt a tug of her own sadness. "I wish I'd known him longer."

"He would be so proud of you."

"And you?" The little girl question was out before she realized it.

Her mother looked surprised. "I've *always* been proud of you."

Emily raised her eyebrows. "Even when I walked out on Carl."

Adrian took a sip of wine. "Well, after a couple of tranquilizers I was very impressed with your courage."

So tactful, Emily thought, and covered her mother's hand. "Thanks, Mom."

Adrian's eyes softened again. "I do worry that your experience with Carl will keep you from—"

"Adrian. Emily." The familiar voice of Millicent Warner scratched across Emily's nerves like fingernails across a chalkboard. Heading straight for their table, Millicent was a terrible gossip, who delighted in repeating bad news to whoever would listen.

"I'm delighted to see you poor things. It's been so long. I've been very worried about you," Millicent said.

Her false sympathy hit Emily like a flat note. Although her instinct was to quietly respond and pray the old biddy left quickly, she stood and gave the gossip a big hug. She smiled for all she was worth. "It's great to see you, Millicent. What a lovely dress. Is that new?" Before Millicent could answer, Emily went on. "It's so sweet of you to be worried, but there's no need. As you can see, my mother is beautiful as ever."

Blinking back her amazement, Millicent braced her hand on the table. "Yes, I can see she's beautiful." She seemed to recover. "But Emily dear, your wedding and Carl." She made a tsking sound. "All your plans. You must be devastated."

Emily beamed. "Oh, no, Millicent. I consider myself damn lucky."

Millicent gasped and gulped and muttered something about meeting her niece. Emily sat down. "Pardon me for swearing."

"Emily," her mother said with a measured glance of approval, "I do believe you've come into your own."

Twelve

A little more than twenty-four hours later, Emily pulled into her driveway. *Her* driveway in Ruxton, North Carolina. She smiled to herself. Her relationship with her mother was better than ever. She liked where she lived. She liked what she was doing. As soon as she caught up with Beau, everything would be right. She still couldn't believe he'd truly thought she wouldn't return.

Grabbing her bag, she walked to her porch and stared in surprise at three florist's arrangements left on a bench. She quickly read the cards and shook her head in wry amusement. The three men Maddie had bought beers for at The Cherry Bomb had sent their regards.

In a rush to reach Beau, she left the flowers on the porch and walked into her house to her phone. She dropped her bag, punched his number and counted the rings. "Pick it up, pick it up, pick it up—"

"Ramsey."

Her heart tightened at the sound of his voice. "Hi. It's Emily. I'm back."

A long silence followed, and she started to get nervous. "Can we get together? Can we—"

"I'm a little busy now. My deputy asked for the evening off, so I need to do a patrol. Maybe later tonight," he said in a distracted tone.

Emily's heart sank to her feet. "Beau, I'm back for good. I'm not fluttering anywhere."

"Good," he said in a noncommittal tone. "If we can't get together tonight, maybe we can try tomorrow. I gotta go. Welcome back," he added, but it sounded like an afterthought.

The disconnecting click vibrated inside her. Emily moved the phone away from her ear and stared at it. She slowly replaced the receiver, but her mind was racing a mile a minute.

What was going on with Beau? Was it merely his persistent belief that she would leave that made him act so distant? Or, she wondered as her stomach tightened with dread, was it something more?

Perhaps he had reconsidered and decided he'd overestimated his feelings for her. Perhaps he'd had enough of her. Her heart clenched at the thought. Perhaps his desire for her had waned. Emily felt a slice of pain cut deep into her soul.

Sinking to her knees on her kitchen tile, she struggled to gain her perspective. Her hands were icy cold with nerves as she reasoned with herself. Beau was human. He was entitled to his own doubts, even if his doubts centered on her. The knowledge grated at her, but she accepted it.

She just wasn't sure what to do about it. Her first instinct was to crawl into a hole and wait. To hurt and hope in private until he could see her for the woman she truly was. Until he was certain of their love.

Everything inside her tightened into a tangled knot of apprehension. She'd spent much of her life waiting and hoping in private, and it hadn't brought her happiness. She'd been fearful and so eager to please that she'd hidden her true self behind a carefully built wall of manners and social courtesy.

Her heart nudged her. Emily was learning that following her heart often led to better places than she'd been. Her hands balled into fists, she asked, "What do I want?"

There was no pause, not the barest hesitation.

She wanted Beau.

Just thinking it and accepting it made everything click into place. Her hands relaxed of their own accord. The tension in her neck eased. Her heart settled into a regular rhythm. When had anything ever felt so right? she wondered, and a powerful resolve set in.

Hours later she finally caught up with Beau at the Happy Hour Bar. More frustrated than anything else, she spotted him talking to Jimmy, the owner. Jimmy was pointing at two men across the room whose voices were getting louder with each passing moment.

Emily walked quickly toward Beau, threading her way through the tables. "Hi," she said. "I really wanted to see you."

Beau looked at her in surprise, then glanced back at Jimmy. "Just a minute," he said to her.

Not the most enthusiastic welcome she'd received, Emily thought, but she could be patient. Even though she'd spent the last few hours on a wild-goose chase trying to find him.

Jimmy looked cross. "Beau, the last time Leroy and T.D. Fitch were in here they did a helluva lot of damage and—"

"Okay, okay." Beau lifted his hand. "I'll go talk to them," he said, and headed toward the two men.

Emily followed Beau. "I can see you're busy, but I hope later we—"

"Welshing on a bet like you always do, Leroy!" The younger of the two men raised his voice.

"I'm not welshing. You're lying. I never called it an official bet. We never shook on it," the tall one said, and got right in the other man's face.

"Who are they?" she asked.

"Fitch brothers," Beau said in disgust. "Can't live together, can't keep from making each other miserable."

"That sounds just like you, slimy as a snake."

"You keep it up and I'm gonna have to teach you a lesson."

Beau sighed. "Okay, boys. That's enough. You're in a public place."

Leroy scowled at Beau. "This is a family matter. It's none of your business."

Emily saw the expression on Beau's face and cringed. If he ever looked at her that way, she would want to hide under the sofa. Apparently Leroy, however, didn't possess a high enough emotional IQ to see he was getting close to a very deep hole.

"It becomes my business when you're disturbing the peace or when one of the business owners calls with a complaint," Beau said in a lethal, low voice.

"Why's Jimmy complaining?" T.D. asked. "We each bought a beer." T.D. looked at his brother and frowned. "*I* bought the beers. Leroy's too damn cheap."

"That does it, T.D., I'm tired of your belly-achin'—"

"You're right, Leroy," Beau said, clearly unwilling to put up with any more foolishness. "That does it. It's time for you to leave."

T.D. tossed Beau an insolent look, but stomped toward the door. "Okay, I'm leavin'. Don't like it here, anyway."

Emily instinctively stepped closer to Beau.

"Me, too," Leroy said. "Right after I—" He swung around and his quick movement alarmed Emily. She stumbled forward.

He rammed his fist toward Beau and missed. She saw it coming, but couldn't move. He whacked Emily in the eye. Stunned, she stopped breathing. The first rush of pain hit her hard, and two seconds later, she fell to the floor. Her entire head throbbed violently, and she immediately covered her eye.

On the fringes of her consciousness, she heard a lot of swearing and some tussling. She would have sworn she heard another body hit the floor, but she was still seeing stars so she couldn't be sure. Beyond her control, moans escaped her mouth.

"I'm gonna kill him," Beau said.

Emily heard more rolling around on the floor.

"You can't kill him," Jimmy said, sounding out of breath. "You're the sheriff."

"Did you see what he did to her? Hit her like she was a man." He swore again, and a few seconds later, she felt his breath on her face.

"Emily." He gently touched her arm.

His voice comforted her in a strange way, but the pain continued unabated. Another moan bubbled out of her mouth. She bit her lip to stop the sounds.

"Emily, sweetheart, look at me," he said, sounding worried, almost desperate. "Let me see."

"No no no no no." She shook her head violently and whimpered.

"Honey, you've gotta let me look at it," he insisted. "C'mon."

She cupped her hand over her throbbing eye and opened the other to look at him. "It really hurts."

Alarm tightened his features. "I know it does, but we have to see if you need a doctor."

"Oh, God, I hope not." She couldn't imagine anyone *touching* her eye. "Please don't touch it," she said. "*Promise* you won't touch it."

He nodded. "I won't touch it. Just let me see it."

She slowly moved her hand away from her already swollen eye.

Beau cringed and swore a blue streak. "I swear Leroy's going to the county jail as soon as he wakes up."

"Wakes up?" she echoed and tried to lift her head.

"I put him to sleep," Beau said. "Don't get up.

Jimmy's wife is taking you home while I get Leroy locked up.''

She felt a strange panic. "Home?"

He looked at her with an expression of complete and absolute possession. "My home. She'll stay with you until I can get there. Get her some ice, Jimmy." He lowered his head and kissed her forehead. "Honey, I'll be back just as soon as I can."

Beau had Leroy's carcass tossed in the county jail in record time considering it was a weekend. He had to resist the urge to pound him into the ground. When the sorry Fitch brother awoke, however, even he was appalled with himself. "Geez, I hit a lady! I can't believe I hit a lady."

Beau still wanted to hurt him, but with Leroy behind bars, his first concern was getting back to Emily. It had scared the spit out of him to see her hit the floor. His heart felt as if it had been ripped to shreds. He was lucky Jimmy had been nearby, or he might have come terribly close to killing Leroy.

A wholly primitive and overwhelming response, it alarmed Beau, because it had sent him momentarily out of control. He was going to have to do something about this, he thought, as he walked through his doorway. He was not rational about Emily.

He nodded toward Thelma, seated on his sofa. "How is she?"

"Resting in your room." Thelma rose. "I gave her a little bite to eat, plenty to drink, and something to work on the swelling. Do you want me to stay?"

Beau shook his head. "No. Thanks for coming."

Thelma smiled and opened the door. "She's a sweet one, Beau. Don't let her get away."

Watching her leave, Beau balled his fists and remembered trying to hang on to the butterflies of his boyhood. His chest felt heavy. He swore under his breath. He rolled his head, trying to relieve the tension in his neck, then walked into his bedroom.

Her one eye met his as he sat down on the bed. She held an ice pack over her injured eye and gave a weak smile. "I never realized proximity to a small-town sheriff could be so adventuresome."

He shook his head. "Emily, we can't go on this way."

Emily felt her heart stop.

He gave a heavy sigh. "I can't keep doing this."

Her whole system went into shock. She couldn't speak.

"The timing sucks. We both know that."

A shaft of pain cut right through the center of her, and she had to bite her lip to keep from crying out. She swallowed hard. "Why? What—" Her voice broke and she couldn't force any more words.

He rose from the bed and began to pace. "I can't keep doing this. I'm like a crazy man. I was ready to *kill* Leroy Fitch. I wanted to kill him. Bad timing or not, I've gotta do something about it."

Her eyes began to tear, stinging her injured eye. She shut them both and took a deep breath. "If you're going to dump me, why did you bring me to your house?" She heard the quaver in her voice and hated it. "You could have just let—"

"Dump you!" he shouted, making her head ring. "Who said anything about dumping you?"

Confused, she clutched her aching head. "You said you can't keep on doing this. You said it's bad timing. What else could you mean?"

She felt the bed dip under his weight. "You're not getting away that easily," he told her. "You blow into town, knock me to my knees, and you think I'm letting you go?"

Still confused, Emily peeked at him with her good eye. "Well, you've been so distant the last couple of days."

"Because I've been scared spitless you were gonna leave. I don't know how you did it, but you filled up my empty place when I didn't know I had one. I sure as hell don't want you to leave."

She felt the first sweet balm of tentative relief. She swallowed over unshed tears and bottled-up emotion. "What are you saying?"

Beau reached for her hand. "Sweetheart, I love you more than I ever thought I'd love anyone. I want you beside me at night and in the morning. I want you with me when the going gets tough. I want to make babies with you. I want to be the man who's with you when you try everything you've always wanted to try, but never have before."

His face was as solemn as a lifelong promise. "Emily, I want to keep you. And I want you to keep me." He swallowed as if he was dealing with his own set of nerves. "I want you to marry me."

Emily blinked. Her heart was hammering a mile a minute. She couldn't believe it. Her ears had heard his words, her mind had processed them, her soul mirrored them, but she couldn't believe it.

"You can say something now," he said roughly.

"I'm stunned," she managed. "We both said it was too soon."

"Will time make you more sure?"

"No," she said, then quickly added. "I'm already sure. I just didn't think you were."

He shook his head and gently pulled her to him. "Is that a yes?"

"Yes," she whispered instantly, her heart full, her mind still trying to catch up. He kissed her, his mouth making the promise again as he tasted her.

She tried to make her brain work. "Do you want to wait a little bit?"

"No," he said, pressing his mouth against her hair.

"Wow."

"Wow what?" He slipped his fingers under her chin and looked at her.

"When I tracked you down tonight, I thought I was going to have to convince you to keep seeing me." She met his amused gaze. "I was going to remind you of the satin sheets."

"Heavy artillery." His mouth eased into a sexy half grin. "That would have worked."

"And then I was going to remind you that I still wanted to light your cigar."

He chuckled. "Emily, I'm surprised at you. Don't you know a man's supposed to save some pleasures for his wife?"

Epilogue

Beau and Emily were married one month later under the big weeping willow tree next to the Methodist church. She wore a new long white gown and everyone swore she looked like a princess. Emily didn't seem to notice, though, because she was so focused on Beau.

It wasn't First Presbyterian in Roanoke, and the reception was not held at the posh Hotel Roanoke. But the people who counted were there: Beau's family and friends, and Emily's mother, stepfather and two best friends, Maddie and Jenna.

Just as Beau and Emily left the reception, a motorcycle whizzed down the street, distracting his bride. Beau covered her eyes with his hand and muttered, "One fantasy at a time." Emily just grinned at him.

Later that night they made slow, sweet love on

black satin sheets, and with very little instruction from her new husband, Emily did a mighty fine job lighting Beau's cigar.

* * * * *

*Don't miss THE TROUBLEMAKER BRIDE,
the second book in Leanne Banks's exciting
series, HOW TO CATCH A PRINCESS,
coming this May, only from Silhouette Desire!*

Coming in March from

▼ SILHOUETTE®

Desire®

HOW TO CATCH A PRINCESS

A fun and sexy new trilogy
by LEANNE BANKS

Meet Emily, Maddie and Jenna Jean. As little girls, each dreamed of one day marrying her own Prince Charming.

Sometimes you have to kiss a lot of frogs before you meet the perfect groom. And three childhood friends are about to pucker up!

THE FIVE-MINUTE BRIDE (#1058, March 1997)—
Runaway bride Emily St. Clair hightails herself off into the arms of a rough-and-rugged sheriff.

THE TROUBLEMAKER BRIDE (#1070, May 1997)—
Expectant single mother Maddie Palmer disrupts the life of the tough loner who helps deliver her baby.

THE YOU-CAN'T-MAKE-ME BRIDE (#1082, July 1997)—
Rule follower Jenna Jean Andrews reluctantly learns to have fun with her rule-breaking childhood nemesis.

Don't miss a single one of these wonderful stories!

HTCP

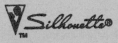

In April 1997
Bestselling Author

DALLAS SCHULZE

takes her Family Circle series to new heights with

In April 1997 Dallas Schulze brings readers a
brand-new, longer, out-of-series title featuring the
characters from her popular Family Circle miniseries.

When rancher Keefe Walker found Tessa Wyndham he
knew that she needed a man's protection—she was
pregnant, alone and on the run from a heartless past.
Keefe was also hiding from a dark past...but in one
overwhelming moment he and Tessa forged a family
bond that could never be broken.

Available in April wherever books are sold.

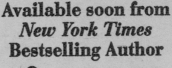

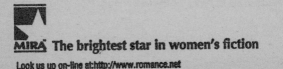

In the tradition of
Anne Rice comes a
daring, darkly sensual
vampire novel by

As a bonus,
you will also receive
a FREE story by
National Bestselling Author
Stella Cameron,
in the same volume.

MAGGIE SHAYNE

BORN IN TWILIGHT

Rendezvous hails bestselling Maggie Shayne's vampire
romance series, WINGS IN THE NIGHT, as
"powerful...riveting...unique...intensely romantic."

Don't miss it, this March, available
wherever Silhouette books are sold.

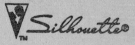

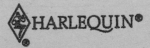